ICE IN THE GUISE OF FIRE

I hope you enjoy!

Nancy Weston

DEDICATION

To the invisible Butte County employees who have lived in
disaster mode for four years through spillway crisis, fire after
fire, including the destruction of the town of Paradise. With
little or no recognition, they are the ones who man the
Emergency Operation Center 24 hours a day during a crisis
or do their regular jobs on the side while processing a
mountain range of paperwork for recovery, restoration, and
reimbursement for their community. These are the unsung
heroes of Butte Strong!

Love and respect you all! I will never forget!

ACKNOWLEDGMENTS

I want to thank Deputy James Norman for sharing his time, experience, and patience.

Also, thanks to my beta reader on this one for their time and diligence, especially Becky not only for her time but for her experience, advice, and counsel.

A special thanks to Claudia Harcourt for her magnificent talent and artistry.

And to Dee for her courage and optimism in the face of adversity.

1

GATHERING STORM

"Ladies and gentlemen, the next wave of the storm is coming into the Bay area earlier than originally anticipated. We are expecting to alter course to avoid the worst of it, but we will be delayed at least forty minutes. Sorry for the inconvenience."

Atticus Flynn, in 1A, glances out the window and sees the moonlight illuminate crests of thick, billowing clouds. This will mean arriving home quite late... rather, quite early in the morning. Accustomed to crafting all aspects of life, he resigns himself to the fact that there are some things that just have to be fate.

He observes his reflection in the window. Handsome. Silver only adds to his image. A distant cloud bursts with light from electricity within. He turns and orders another drink, inhales deeply, and reminds himself that in all other aspects of life, everything is unfolding perfectly. As anticipated. He sighs in surrender of this small point. He has other contemplations of far greater significance. He turns his mind to them and leaves the storm and the aircraft to the pilots.

Eli Lucas motors up the driveway at his home in Peregrine Hills above Moluku Lake. Eli's hair is thin; he's portly. He is the partner of Atticus Flynn, and together, they own and operate Eagle's Nest, the exclusive resort in the town of Moluku Lake. The lake is nestled in the Sierra Nevada, the mountainous spine of California, and a border between the two states.

The town and lodge are intertwined in an exclusive culture of ease, pleasure and privacy. It is where the wealthy, seeking something interesting and accommodating, go-to holiday year-round. In winter: skiing and winter carnivals. In summer: boating and gourmet festivals. But one way or the other, if you are anyone at all in Northern Cali, you have property in Moluku Lake, or you stay at Eagle's Nest: the epitome of self-indulgent *nesting*!

It is winter. The resort is experiencing waves of snow—setting records. The Pineapple Express, always welcome, is lined up on the north state this year, so Eli is guiding his vehicle down a canyon of snow with storm clouds for a ceiling. Just starting to snow and bitterly cold for the region. It will likely snow all night.

This will be difficult for the single largest social event of Moluku Lake tomorrow night at the lodge: the Art Council annual fundraiser. But then, this is Moluku Lake, and nothing impedes the opulent and prominent from displaying their wealth and grandeur, not here. Of course, their celebrity is not always celebrated in pop culture. The rich and famous frequent, but it is the cloistered financial dynasties that are the inner circle of this town. The gala is the spectacle of the year, and this year, it is a masque ball. The snow crews are busy and poised for more.

Reaching the house, Eli secures his Sequoia inside the garage. Then, with a quickened pace, he heads into the mudroom of the house he shares with his wife, Grace, hangs his parka, and removes his boots. Although Eli runs the day-to-day operations at the lodge, once the day is over, his thoughts turn exclusively to home and the delights that await him in the arms of Grace.

Grace is younger than Eli by a decade. She is fifty-two going on forty, and if the cosmetic surgeons in San Francisco have free reign, she will remain forty forever. Eli and Grace have been married for seventeen years. Nonetheless, Grace is determined to be Eli's trophy wife—keep his focus and never worry about losing Eli to a younger, more alluring woman. Especially since he works in the middle of youth, swank, and glamour.

Eli is not handsome, but he is cute in a cuddly way, and very wealthy. Grace enjoys sex and spends her day planning the entertainment for the evening, including all the toys and accouterments of adventurous pleasure.

Tonight, Eli enters to dimmed lighting, fire crackling, candles, Johnny Mathis on the Bose, and incense floating lightly on the air. Sure enough, there is Grace in the great room, spread out on the faux skin rug with nothing on but a white pearl thong pressing softly into her smooth pink skin, pearl-crusted pasties on her nipples. Champagne is chilled, glasses filled, a caviar platter, and to the side, chocolate-dipped strawberries. Since Grace has perfectly round, firm breasts and shapely legs, Eli is enthusiastic from the moment he first sees the candlelight flicker over her hills and valleys.

He inhales the sandalwood, coyly smiles with a slight crank of his head to the left and begins to peel the day away: sweater, tie, shirt... Grace takes care of the rest. Up and moving, she loosens, tugs with playful force, and makes every touch a promise of play and the dissipation of the day's stress. Eli's hands pulse electric messages to and from his sacral chakra as he enjoys the perfect sensations of Grace's flesh in his hands. Eli doesn't know what a chakra is. But Grace does.

Logan Malloy inhales deeply with self-satisfied indulgence. She has followed her flawless instincts and caught a far more prized trophy than she originally stalked.

She ignores the snow falling outside, sees her own reflection in the plate glass window before her, and takes down the last sip of her latest martini. Amid her gloating, she observes that she is alluring, dressed only in her sheerest nightclothes. She gives herself a half-grin, and her eyes respond with a half wink. This is a night of triumph! One which she has waited a long time to enjoy, and it is not over yet.

Behind her, she senses movement from her silenced quarry, to whom she has turned her back as if to dismiss further discussion or resistance. Ready to *reel in*, she turns.

She sees a gun pointed at her heart, and awareness instantly reduces to the dark width of the barrel. She wants to utter a cry but is startled speechless by eyes, fierce, piercing, and committed—*not* what she was anticipating.

The sudden shift from predator to prey creates a disconnect in her brain. Instead of sound, only a sudden violent inhale can be mustered. Adrenaline explodes from her glands as her hands rise in reflex to the danger, but at that exact moment, there is a spark, an explosion.

She feels a painless thud in her chest, a seizing sensation, followed by a white-hot deep burn. In a desperate move, she commands her hand to grasp yet does not know if it obeys as a loss of sensation in her arms, legs, is followed by the inability to remain upright.

On the floor, she is looking up into the face of her assailant. The room closes into a small aperture as her brain suffers oxygen deprivation. She sees ghostly images, scenes flashing in her mind, interfering with her focus, consciousness. The last image her brain records is the indifferent face of her murderer as she grapples, vacillates between gasps of incredulity and the terror of drifting, helpless, fading, and dying.

The assailant looks down placid cheeks without moving, as if the scene is not worthy of the effort to reposition one's head, demeaning the carnage on the floor as beneath contempt. The wind outside is gusting, working the weakened plate glass window. The penetrated crack pattern hangs together, suspended in its frame. Until it cannot. The small geometric pieces of glass rain down on the floor and the last flickers of a life. The killer barely seems to notice the crash—fitting punctuation. A small tight smile almost emerges. There is passion, but it is brittle like icicles and frigid like the wind blowing in the gaping window. "Time to go. Ta-ta now."

Betsy Hall is a waitress at Oeufs et Crème, the best café in town, located on the ground floor in Eagle's Nest Lodge. The café serves what could be termed French comfort food, and everyone loves it! The café opens at 6:00 a.m. and is packed until 10:00 a.m. Betsy likes to work the morning shift because it is busy, and the time passes easily. But she has to rotate her hours because the café is open until ten in the evening seven days a week. Today she starts at eleven; then she will cover lunch and the slower afternoon.

By evening, she will work the benefit event in the ballroom but not as a waitress. Betsy likes to work the big events: see the people in their gorgeous outfits, rubbing elbows with the power pack. This year it is a masque ball, and so the elaborate decadence will be all the more fascinating. She fantasizes that one of them will take an interest in her aspirations as a singer. Betsy dreams of a singing career and fame... someday. Despite the fact that she is good but not extraordinary.

For now, a promotion to the wait staff at Aigle Noir, the exclusive restaurant upstairs, is her goal. Aigle Noir is only open from 6:00 p.m. to midnight Thursday, Friday, Saturday, and Sunday for brunch. The hours are less, but the wages are better and the tips obscene.

As it is, Betsy works five and six days a week, and the hours shift and complicate her life. The constant shifting of hours allows flexibility in caring for her six-year-old daughter, but sometimes it also creates problems fitting everything into her schedule, and she feels she works to support her sitter. The constrained hours at Aigle Noir would be much better. The hours and the money could make her life as a single mom much easier. Meanwhile, Betsy takes extra work when she can fit it in.

One extra gig is cleaning house for the owner of the local newspaper, Logan Malloy. It's not much of a newspaper. It is more like the local gossip rag with news on the side. Of course, everyone reads it. It has a mail distribution all the way to the Bay Area, and those who frequent the resort get it electronically by subscription.

Malloy loves juicy stories and has been known to shade or embellish the truth to stir trouble or protect a "friend." The ulterior purpose is not always obvious; her allegiance is capricious but always of value to Logan Malloy.

Everyone in town knows that it is a mistake to get on Logan's list. She is ruthless and not shy of printing stories to ruin this one or elevate that one. Logan Malloy is a cold-blooded scalawag. Nonetheless, cleaning the Malloy house is a nice piece of income for Betsy!

She arrives at Malloy's home, crunching snow as she drives up to the front entrance. It is below freezing this morning, so Betsy zips her parka, jumps out of her Escort, and moves quickly to the front door with the wind slicing at her cheeks. She attempts to put her key in the lock, but it is already turned, and the door opens. Odd. She steps inside and removes her snow boots. The house is abnormally cold inside, and she feels the wind blowing from *inside* the house as she enters.

"Ms. Malloy?" No answer. "Hello? Anyone here?" Sometimes Logan Malloy works from her home office, but usually, she is at the newspaper, and early. This lets Betsy get there, clean, and get back before her daughter awakes to get ready for school. She moves forward to gain a better vantage point of the large open living room from the split-level entry.

A body is sprawled on the hardwood in front of the floor-to-ceiling windows, one of which is shattered and lying on the floor all around. The wind has free rein of the house, and the body is covered in a crusted layer of snow. Paper is scattered, books are blown open and flapping, a glass is broken on its side next to a platter of cheese also covered by snow, and crackers are flung across the granite coffee table, leaving lumps under the dusting next to shriveled frozen fruit.

A full minute before Betsy can bring herself to think, she blinks and actually looks at the scene before her. She realizes that the white area rug is stained deep, dark red... blood. Her breaths shorten and grow shallow. Again, stunned, transfixed now on the thick crimson pool, ice crystals forming at its edges.

It is another minute for the fear to grip her. She inhales as her brain reboots. It occurs to Betsy that she should not take another step or touch anything. "What would Gibbs do?" She reaches into her jeans pocket and pulls out her cell phone. She debates who to call first. Then dials.

"What is the nature of your emergency?"

2

ICE SCULPTURES

Lieutenant Lauren Riley loves the drive from Butte County to Moluku and has made the trek many times. The wind has blown a hole in the storm, and sunlight is strobing through the pine trees to shine and then not, creating shadows on the thick new layer of snow.

Lieutenant Riley has strong features and bronze skin, black eyes, and black hair that softly hints at a wave as it graces her shoulder. Today, she has it French braided to the back of her head and snug at the nape. She and her partner, Deputy Kevin Rodriguez, are driving toward Peregrine Hills, the Moluku Lake suburb where the wealthy and influential have their mansions on the west ridge.

"Oowey! Look at the size of that eagle!" says Lieutenant Riley.

"That's a big one!" Deputy Rodriguez responds.

"Probably a female."

"How can you know that?"

"The females are significantly larger in size. And they have longer talons and bigger beaks. My mother says females are more aggressive and ferocious. Birds of prey hang here near the fish creek. The fish that get through the locks and tumble down that creek sometimes are stunned and float at the mouth for a couple of seconds. The birds swoop and grab them up. That's why this is Moluku Lake. Even before the dams, when the waters were wild, the Indians knew that's where to come stock food supplies in the mountains."

"Ya don't say."

"That's why they named it. She says long ago, in the gold rush days, it was the last home of the Maidu. *Moluku*," she said in the voice of the People, "is the Maidu word for *eagle*."

"Haven't known you for long, but you seem to know a lot about Indian lore and seem to know your way around this resort."

"Well, I am Maidu." Riley cast a look at her partner and gave a smile. "My mother is on the Council. My middle name is Toyá. Something my mother gave me to always remind me who I am. But it was she who told me to go and find my way outside the tribe. She doesn't have a lot of good things to say about a woman's prospects in her world."

"If she's on the Council, she must have fared well."

"My mother has a lot of grit and fight in her. I guess she didn't want me to have to fight as hard." She laughs. "So I get a degree and go into law enforcement to fight a different kind of battle. I guess it is just in our nature—confrontation, battling." Riley knows she has a warrior inside of her. But she prefers to put out her intellectual self and save her pugilism for those moments when absolutely necessary. Riley knows her mother, on the other hand, relishes the battle—both intellectual strategy as well as the actual fight.

"And so, today, I am back home." Lieutenant Riley is smiling big and joyously. She knows Sheriff Noble gave her this assignment because of her connection to the tribe in this town, to her mother. She doesn't care. This is a great opportunity. She knows she can accomplish many things on this mission. She will apply herself, all of herself: her strength, wit, and instincts. Inside, she feels as if this is the chance she has waited for. Now that she is a lieutenant, she doesn't get to investigate, with few chances to actually be in the field. But this one is special. Potential. And tricky. She will have to keep her balance. Maybe that is why he sent her. To see if she can keep her balance. It will be important, one way or the other.

The two deputies arrive at their destination. They park on the road where other vehicles from the Moluku Police Department and Butte Corner are parked and walk in on the flagged path set far to the side, preserving the scene dusted in snow.

"Well, it looks like we have our murder for the year. There's a woman in there shot in the chest, dead. Logan Malloy herself," the police officer on the scene says with a laugh as he greets them at the front door. "BCSO, right?"

"Yes. Riley!" She extends her hand, shaking the officer's. "Interesting. Deputy Kevin Rodriguez," she says with a turn and gesture. They both nod.

"She must have *really* pissed someone off!"

"She was good at that," Lieutenant Riley acknowledges with a sigh and slight shake of her head. Even a county away, Logan Malloy's reputation meanders, and some subscribe to her paper.

"Yeah. But murder? Was anyone *that* upset with her? It's just a gossip rag," Riley's partner, Rodriguez, says.

"Someone obviously was. Cause she's dead!" the Moluku police officer said with a scoffing laugh.

Riley's eyes snap in the direction of the officer and darken a bit to convey her disapproval of the second piece of flippant humor. Lauren Toyá Riley has a pleasant face with a broad smile, bright teeth, and a dimple in the left cheek. It pulls you in—unless she draws in her brows. When she does that, her face quickly shifts to menacing. "Drugs? Burglary?" she says, shifting the subject.

"No. The place is a mess, but it isn't stripped like it would be if it were a burglary, and no paraphernalia—unless you count the giant bottle of gin."

"OK. Enough speculating. Let's do our job," Riley states. "I understand the housekeeper found the body?"

"Yes. She called it in as soon as she arrived. We took her statement and sent her home. Pretty shook up."

"So the tire tracks on the drive must be hers."

"Yes. There are other marks underneath, but those were covered by snow and then driven over by the housekeeper. Probably no useable tread left. But we'll check it out, digitize anything we find usable."

"Please verify if she gets her drive plowed and when. So someone drove here after the storm last night. Possibly more than one. Thanks."

The two deputies proceed inside the house. The flat screens are untouched, so is the Alexa and other fast-cash items. But there is a mess. Not just the body, the window and the wind. Someone had been searching for something without regard for the disarray they created. "Interesting," she repeats. She pauses for a moment and looks at the gaping frame that held the window. "Interesting."

The biggest mess is in the office, just off the living room. Computer is still there, on the floor, smashed. At the edge of the carpet in the office is an evidence marker. Riley pauses and squats down for a closer look. It is a depression on the carpet. There are others. The snow has made it this far, but just barely. What the forensic team has caught is a slight bit of red as if someone with a hint of blood on their shoe, not completely removed across the floor, stepped here when entering the office. The blood has frozen, leaving the cells to clump a little. So easy to miss. But they didn't.

All the papers from the desk are scattered as if someone has sifted through them, looking for something and letting fly anything that did not fit the search criteria. The wind has made it worse. The in basket is upside down on the floor, and there are files strewn, blown across the floor where the laptop is lying, busted. "The question I have is, was she the one searching?"

"Don't think so. That tiny bit of blood could indicate that the search came after the victim was shot."

"Then was she killed because she wouldn't give it up, or killed so the search could begin?"

"Either? Someone in a hurry. Needed to find whatever and get out. I want the computer."

"Sorry, ma'am, but it is busted up pretty bad."

"Take it anyway—especially the hard drive."

"Drive's gone."

"Any other drives?"

"None that we've found."

"Very interesting."

After documenting the details of the body, the ME sweeps the snow off of it. Logan Malloy is wearing a full-length negligee under a silk kimono: very sheer. It was hot pink, but now, soaked in blood, it appears grotesque.

The crime scene team is still taking photographs in the office. The living room is tagged with markers everywhere. The coffee table is a frozen jigsaw puzzle of snow, ice, lumps, bumps, and an ice-cold bottle of wine, uncorked, almost full, so it did not blow over. The coroner is packing up and the body about to be bagged. "Come look at this. Before we bag her up."

The deputies stand over the body: frozen, pale, eyes dark with fully blown pupils, riveted behind a cloudy veil. The hand holds something, withered, shriveled. Yet even in death, Malloy's fist holds it firm. Odd.

Riley thinks to herself, looking into the eyes of death, "*If only we could see the film of what those eyes last captured. What were you staring at, Ms. Malloy?*" She looks carefully at the face and sees something frozen into the features. Even in death, there is a hint of that last moment.

"She was facing her killer, through and through. Bullet's probably out there in the snow. They'll find it. No casing in here," the coroner says. "Tidy. Or a revolver."

"TOD, Doctor?"

"The cold will have to be factored in, but I think it is safe to say twelve-ish hours ago. Rigor is engaged, but there is also tissue freezing in the extremities. I'll be able to zero in on a more exact time when I can calculate the cold into the equation more precisely. For this, I need to get to the morgue in Butte County. They don't have any facilities in Quincy. Good thing the highway is fairly clear for now 'cause this one's top priority. Might give me the window I need to get down the hill before the next storm hits. I hear it's going to be a doozy."

"What's that in her hand?"

"Yes. That is what I wanted you to see. It's a stem and part of a flower. Probably came from the vase of flowers that was on the table behind the sofa, in front of the window. She was standing there when she fell. Blood spatter puts her right next to them. The cut crystal vase was too heavy for the wind to knock over. Wind did its damage to whatever was in the vase. Not much left now but shriveled stems. I can tell you more. We bagged all the withered remains of whatever it was. Her grip would have relaxed a bit at the moment of death. But then rigor would have stiffened her grip again. That's what you are seeing right now. Just rigor mortis... and cold. I just wanted you to take note."

"Flowers of some sort. She could have been putting them in the vase and had the last one in her hand."

"The water's icy now, but it's cloudy. They've been in that vase for more than a day."

"She could have been rearranging them."

"Or she could be trying to tell us something."

"Could."

"Probably nothing."

"Yes. Probably nothing."

Lieutenant Riley slowly pivots herself around to take one last look at the living room. She pauses one more moment to look at the gaping hole. "Did something go through that window? To take it down like that?"

The ME replies, "You mean besides the bullet?"

"Why did it fall?"

"Ask Chen."

She sees the disarray, but more, observes the style of the room. Modern, expensive. It is not at all delicate or ornate. It is actually austere, lacking in amenities, adornments. There are some books. A few civic recognition plaques. Electronics. Furnishings. Riley tries to put a word to it. Like no one really "lived" here. She goes into the kitchen. It is neat. She opens the refrigerator. It is sparsely populated with white wine, cheeses, some pâté, and condiments. Something long past edible in a Styrofoam container.

"Did you get the trash?"

The Forensic Tech responds, "Yes, ma'am. All of it."

"This is going to leave a wake!" Riley says to Rodriguez. Her partner cocks his head to the side and nods.

Of course it will. Logan Malloy was not loved, had no family to speak of, and will not be mourned, but she was powerful, feared, and a huge force in Lake Moluku. "How do we find a murderer when everyone in the community is a suspect? Was there anyone she didn't take a shot at during her reign?" Riley decides it may be easier to eliminate alibis for the most obvious suspects and see who is left on the list after that. Heavy sigh.

The mayor of Moluku Lake clomps into the Butte County Sheriff's Office with authority and grabs a chair without being invited to do so. Mason Oeillet is a bully and an oaf but is also from a wealthy, influential family, a force to be reckoned with and feared for his temper and ability to upset apple carts and get his way. Sheriff Jason Noble knows that it is as much his job to keep peace among the people of his towns as it is to keep order. But Moluku Lake is outside his jurisdiction.

The call had come early in the morning. Plumas County is not crime-free, but it is largely about domestic violence, substance abuse, and the occasional dispute turned physical. Plumas' topography is the Sierra Nevada's. It has a population of less than twenty thousand. They are not equipped to handle a first-degree homicide. Interagency collaborations are common in rural regions to leverage limited resources.

Sheriff Noble is not surprised by the mayor's visit, just apprehensive. Mason Oeillet is menacing, corrupt, and always making a move. His arrival on *this* morning, with news of Logan Malloy's demise crackling on small-town communication—and at the speed of light—is somewhat predictable but no less repulsive.

While the seat of his pants is still on the way to the chair, Oeillet bellows, "Well, I hope you are going to look at Eagle's Nest for this! Everyone knows that Atticus Flynn and Logan were at each other's throats over the casino deal! She told me she was working on a piece that would take care of Flynn's objections and lock this deal down! So no one had a better motive. Questioned him yet?"

"He was out of town until early this morning. But I'll go up this morning and drop by the lodge. I already talked with Chief Billings and dispatched two of my deputies, and one is an ace detective, a lieutenant so big guns on this. We're on it, Mason. Back off, OK?"

"You better get up there before the storm sets in. Out of town? You mean, out plotting and planning to shut Logan's exposé down. He was there. It was him who shot her! Had to be!"

"Not if he wasn't there!"

"He could have bought it!"

"I think it would be best not to leap to conclusions, Mason. If that's what happened, the evidence will show us the way to make a solid arrest. Meanwhile, it is murder and under investigation. No one is above suspicion, not even you, drilling with a fine point on the subject. She was pretty hard on you during the election, and it is common knowledge that you two didn't get along. In terms of who had cause, Mason, you are high on the list!"

"I'll admit it. I won't miss that witch, but I had no call to kill her. Besides, as long as she was about to torpedo Flynn and his case against the casino, why would I want her dead?"

"I didn't say you did. I said we'll be keeping open minds, and until the pieces come together, no one is in the clear. Logan had a lot of dirt on everyone. Maybe Flynn is not the only one she was about to torpedo."

The sheriff allows his eyes to settle on Mason Oeillet's eyes. He decides to hold back but wants to set the mayor back a bit. It is just as common knowledge that the mayor is in bed with the local tribe and will probably benefit from the new casino in ways that might not stand scrutiny. Everyone knows it. So far, no one can prove it.

There had been ugly outbursts at Council meetings. Scenes and hubbub at City Hall, talk of a grand jury investigation. This has been simmering for months. Perhaps Logan had found a way to prove the mayor's complicity in illegal activities. It would be just like her to take money from the casino people to get Flynn while simultaneously blackmailing Oeillet with exposure of some proof she'd finagled.

And then there's Oeillet's philandering, with any attractive woman he could seduce with his money, influence, or bullish behavior. But that's cheap thrills in Moluku Lake and not big news. Provender for Malloy's paper, though. On the other hand, Sheriff Noble knows that everyone up there is doing someone or something that Malloy would find fodder.

The sheriff believes that this mess does not need to be further complicated by the local politics. He also knows that the chances are, local politics are exactly what this is all about. He does not look forward to untangling this murder, though he knows that is exactly what he was asked to do.

Butte is not the crime capital of the state, but it is more experienced and better resourced than several of the adjacent jurisdictions. It has more than ten times the population of Plumas and often steps in and helps out surrounding law enforcement agencies—some of which are smaller and less experienced. Some of them used to be part of a larger Butte County before the split of jurisdiction.

Jason and his department also have an outside perspective. Moluku Lake is a powder keg, and now someone has lit the fuse. Moluku Lake police want nothing to do with this conundrum. But Jason Noble doesn't need to take center stage. At least, not yet. He has sent his best to handle things.

The mayor leans forward for emphasis and to raise his mass from the chair, pursing his lips and scowling. "I want that arrogant asshole Flynn held accountable! Get it done!"

Sheriff Noble decides he's said enough. He thinks to himself, *"I don't take orders from you, asshole,"* but is silent as the mayor abruptly turns and leaves. Jason inhales deeply and lets it out very slowly through his pursed lips. He also knows there is a huge event in Moluku Lake tonight. Another sigh.

The café is bustling, but the lodge in general is quiet early in the morning. Eli Lucas never arrives before nine and usually around ten o'clock. He and Grace typically wake up to their own shared internal clock and make love, and then Grace makes breakfast. They do not interrupt their mornings with phone calls or television. This morning, Eli pulls Grace in for a morning kiss. Morning breath is not pleasant, but it *is* intimate. It is not shared with anyone other than lovers, so it is subliminally erotic to Eli. A thought of last night comes into his mind. "So, Grace, what do those pearls feel like down there?"

She snuggles in and emits a muffled giggle. "They open me up and gently massage. They move as I move and make me eager for you, your hands, and other things." She wiggles in his arms just a bit, pressing herself into him. She doesn't bother to mention that they can also pinch.

"Ummm," he moans with sensations as he prepares to partake in Grace once more. He doesn't consciously think of it, but somewhere else in his mind, he is processing his gratitude, and deep in that thought is his secret wish that his business partner knew what he had, how she makes him feel. Nothing that Atticus could buy, own, or wear could rival this.

Today, Grace makes waffles. She is transparent in a negligee, and he smiles as he leaves.

When Eli gets in his car, the murder of Logan Malloy is all over the local radio station, and it is a rude shock to his sated, mellow mood as he drives down the hill toward town. He is alarmed. He pushes away uncomfortable possibilities and concerns. He shakes his head several times. Not that he cares about Malloy. She was an odious piece of work. But who could have done this? Small town. So interlaced. What does this mean?

Arriving at the lodge, Eli is greeted with the smell of maple syrup, bacon, hollandaise, breads, and espresso—sensational! Usually, Eli grabs a croissant and an espresso. But that is far from his thoughts when the Oeufs et Crème manager assails him, exclaiming that they are short a waitress, and Betsy can't come in.

"She always works! That's odd."

"Apparently, she found Malloy's body early this morning! She's upset. Said she'd be here later, which is good because she is also scheduled to work the big event this evening."

"Huh, really. Well, that's understandable. Tell Jayden about it. That's his problem."

Eli turns to the elevator, thinking he should do something supportive for Betsy, pondering that up to the top floor and into his office. Atticus was traveling. Back last night. Probably won't be in for hours. Eli places his hands flat on his desk and takes in an extended breath. His eyes are moving back and forth over his desk, and his mind is whirling. It is settling on him. Logan Malloy is dead. He huffs an exhale. Well, who won't be relieved about that? He doesn't feel relief. Something is nagging him.

Days ago, before Atticus left, there was an ugly episode in Aigle Noir. Atticus and Logan had a private meeting while the restaurant was closed. Eli walked in at the end, and Logan was saying, "Drop it or else, Flynn! I mean it! Believe me, you will sincerely regret pressing this forward!"

Atticus had stood there with his chin upturned, looking down his face with a smirk, his eyes squinted slightly, and his teeth set firmly. He had glared at Logan's backside as she departed and Eli arrived. When Eli had looked to his business partner for an explanation, all Atticus would say was, "Someday, that harridan is going to get what's coming to her!"

Eagle's Nest, the heart of the town, is built on the western upslope of Moluku Lake, directly below the dramatic hills and its ski lifts. From the chairs and runs on the hill, you can see the lodge and a gorgeous view of the lake, the ridge to the east. The runs weave across the hills but all culminate in a small meadow, the back yard of the lodge. People ski right up to the patio, or when it snows a lot, like now, up to the main deck for a Kioki coffee or a shot of Yukon Jack. At this time of year, the lake is partially frozen, where it is shallow, around the edges, the docks, and piers, so the watercraft are all put up. Now it is iceboating and skating. Moluku Lake is a year-round operation.

Eli and Atticus have it all in their pocket because they own the entire ski resort, including the exclusive lodge with its bay, docks, ballroom, performance venue, restaurants, spa, and suites. It is booked in advance all year. They charge premium rates and have few, if any, vacancies.

Atticus is the visionary. He worked with architects to completely revamp the old lodge that the partners purchased over twenty years ago. Out with the log cabin, taxidermy motif, and in with the redwood, glass, and granite. Atticus traveled all over, finding unique and spectacular art pieces for the walls. He inserted interesting architectural styles, like a two-story engineered wall of glass, slabs of black onyx sculpture in the lobby as pillars for the balcony, and the massive circular fireplace in the main lounge with the copper flue that rises up and through the ceiling. Beneath the copper flue, the gas flames emerge through cobalt blue fire glass so that it appears that the flames are coming out of ice. The effect is captivating, mesmerizing.

Atticus is smart. Everything is energy efficient—even though that just offsets some of the not-so-efficient features, like the glass walls and high ceilings. Nonetheless, the field of solar panels, the geothermal cooling in the summer, and the new hydrothermal plant up at the hot springs all contribute to the impression that Moluku Lake and especially the lodge are on the leading edge of carbon-conscious energy consumption. And, as in most things, appearance and marketing are what count.

Atticus saw to every detail of the renovation and still oversees constant updates. He travels the country, world, has a flare, an eye, and a sense of quality, exacting in his expectations. Atticus leaves the operation entirely to Eli.

Eli has no distinguishing personal style and no flare. But he knows the hospitality business, detail-oriented and good with his people. Eli lavishes praise when due and discusses performance issues in private. His staff is loyal and disciplined. He runs a tight ship and asserts customer-focused quality in every single transaction.

After all the years, Eli can do all this without a lot of personal stress. He has built a competent team, and they know what they are doing. Eli just makes sure they have what they need to get the job done and stays involved but not in their way. And that works well because Grace likes Eli home routinely and on time, something Eli already anticipates even as he drives in to work in the mornings. Eli also has Atticus' back because Atticus tends to walk a fine edge between a gentleman with immaculate style and grace and an incendiary provocateur.

Conversely, Atticus Flynn does not keep regular hours. He enjoys travel and an eclectic schedule. He and his wife, Marie Oeillet Flynn, are the resort's power couple. Mrs. Flynn, unlike Atticus, is restrained in her role as the social empress of Moluku Lake. And that is what she is, crowned and revered. She is the anchor to Atticus and his high-flying flair. The Flynns live in an elite mansion, and people actually spend time angling to get on the Flynn party list.

Mrs. Flynn sits on the Moluku Lake Arts Council and quietly commands the town's social agenda. She tolerates, rather than envies, the obvious sensual style of Grace Lucas, since Grace *is* her husband's partner. Mrs. Flynn comes from money. Old money in the Valley. Power and influence are far better than sexual allure. Tending to this profile, this image, is her primary occupation and singular purpose. It sustains her.

Together, the Flynns are stunning. Their contrast makes their public persona more appealing. It pleases the Flynns greatly that the rest of Moluku Lake measures their rank and position at least in part by whether or not they can get the Flynns to attend one of their events. Of course, Atticus is frequently out of town, and when he is in town, he is often busy and distracted. This has never bothered Marie. She is also busy. So their appearances together are fairly rare but exquisite and riveting.

On this foreboding morning, Atticus arrives, earlier than Eli expected. He is dressed in his usual impeccable fashion: crisp suit, signature hand-tied bow tie, and a white carnation in his buttonhole. He is followed by an entourage from the kitchen: an ice bucket with a magnum of Bollinger, two glasses, a bouquet of long-stem red roses, and a large vase. "Water the roses and pour the champagne, please!"

Eli hears him coming down the hall and joins Atticus in his office. Eli observes that Atticus is handsome, dashing, and today, he has a particular twinkle in his bright blue eyes.

"We are celebrating! The wicked witch is dead, and so is that casino! It's only a 2004 vintage, but the day is early. Drink up, Eli!"

"I don't think you should be celebrating, Atticus. What will people think? And I doubt the casino is dead. Delayed at best."

"People? What people? I *am* celebrating. One giant obnoxious threat just bit the dust! I'm sorry, Eli, I will not feign grief or pretend I am not delighted! Dead enough for today! Tomorrow will take care of itself. It always has."

"Thank you anyway, Atticus. I don't like to drink during the day. It just makes the day... long." Eli didn't bother to mention that as soon as he has a glass of wine, he warms, thinks of Grace, and gets a chubby. Not conducive to a day's work—that comes later. "Why the roses?"

"Very well. I will drink it myself. And then I have a meeting. I'll be busy till this evening." He looks over at Eli, sensing the disapproval but amused more than anything. "The roses? Well, I love flowers, and today, I want to be surrounded by all the things I love. Special, exquisitely special day."

Eli returns to his office, but his sense of discomfort is rising to a new level such that he actually forms the thought, *"Could Atticus have done this thing? Could he have anything to do with it? No. He's too smart for that."*

Jayden Listeri earned a degree in hospitality management before a Grand Diplôme de Cuisine et de Pâtisserie Le Cordon Bleu in Paris. These credentials, plus a glowing recommendation, earned him a start as sous chef in an upscale restaurant in New York. But Jayden was not ready to settle for chef and isn't ready to settle for executive chef. He wants to run a gourmet empire. He envisions himself a celebrity chef with international food lines and global acclaim. He is young with a plan!

Eagle's Nest affords Jayden an opportunity to design, plan, and manage bars, restaurants, and every aspect of the resort's hospitality as it relates to cuisine. It is a glorious launching point.

He has implemented summer festivals that celebrate everything from wine to charcuterie. He brought several fine stores to Moluku Lake, carrying local wines, beers, and exotic whiskeys; cheeses and terrines; olive oils and balsamic vinegars, and holds a small but influential position in each of them. They fit in with the snobbish tastes of the clientele that frequent the resort, and Listeri has become quite the epitome of *la bonne vie*.

Meanwhile, he indulges his other passions. Jayden is known as the top of the gay food chain in Moluku Lake. It is said that he has an appetite for every gorgeous young man in town and a fleet of lovers. His dress is flashy, and his style is edgy and decadent. He enjoys a lucrative income and spends it on his wardrobe, his loft, and ostentatious cars. He enjoys a certain amount of gravity in his universe, drawing in a circle in Moluku Lake as well as routine orbits from San Francisco's galaxy of the culinary bleeding-edge trend and style setters.

This morning, while listening to the news, he is ordering etched crystal port glasses from England, and a third division of his concentration is listening to the Glen Miller Orchestra on vinyl. Jayden is attired in silk pajama bottoms and a matching robe, open, barefooted, unshaven with tousled hair. He is munching maple-glazed clumps of granola and sipping thick, sweet espresso. The knock jars him from his multifaceted preoccupation.

"Yes? How can I help you, ah, Officer?" Jayden lowers the noise volume with a word.

"Lieutenant, actually, Lieutenant Riley, and this is my partner, Deputy Rodriguez. We'd like a few minutes of your time."

"Certainly. What is this about, if I may inquire?"

"Logan Malloy."

"Well, of course, I've heard. And you beat a line to my door. How droll. I can't imagine what I can tell you, but please, come in."

The deputies enter Listeri's loft overlooking the main drag of Moluku Lake, complete with a view over the top of the buildings across the street to the ice-cold lake and the eastern mountains. Main Street is decorated with festive ribbon medallions on each lamp post and pine garlands heavy with snow draped from one side to the other. Colorful banners and flags celebrate this event or that shoppe.

The downtown is a patchwork of early twentieth-century brick buildings—carefully preserved—and some well-kept mid-century chalet-style structures. They house bars, restaurants, small boutique hotels, overpriced furniture and jewelry stores, and beauty, ice cream, and massage parlors, while the upstairs are the offices of lawyers, investment brokers, and dentists, as well as art galleries and upscale apartments, like Listeri's. The perfect postcard view.

The walls of the loft are bold neutral colors and set off large, colorful, geometric acrylic paintings as well as a replica bronze of *David*. The contrast of modern and classic is reflected in all of Jayden's selections throughout the living room.

Lieutenant Riley smells the expresso and sees the small glass cup sitting by Listeri's computer. She observes all this in the context of the complicated young man before her. She also notes that although Listeri is well known for his showy appearance, this room is striking more for the artwork on the wall than the understated furnishings. She decides that Listeri might himself be a set of contradictions and files this away for future reference.

"Did you know Logan Malloy?"

"Everyone knew her."

"Everyone knew of her. Not everyone knew her personally. She recently wrote a rather scathing review of you personally. So I am asking if you knew her."

"Malloy did not write that. Elyse James probably wrote it, and Logan published it in her ridiculous rag."

"We visited the paper this morning and learned that Malloy actually authored that little article. And I can't imagine you found it flattering to be referred to as a homosexual cliché. So maybe you will answer my question. What was your relationship with Logan Malloy?"

"Lieutenant, I ran into her at my restaurants. We spoke. We did not have a relationship."

"Where were you between ten and midnight last night, Mr. Listeri?"

"I was here. Busy. Alone."

"No alibi?"

"Had I known I would need one, I assure you, I would have one."

"What did you think of her?"

"A love-hate thing, really. Logan loved to skewer me in one article and praise me in another. In that same edition, in the "Chair Five" section, she praised me for my stock of exotic vodkas. Besides, no publicity is bad, and in the end, it did me good rather than harm. I found her... amusing."

"Then you will miss her contributions to this little community?"

"Depends on who takes over at the paper, and I hope it is not that obvious and obscene little gossip columnist protégé of hers, Elyse James. It also depends on whether or not I continue to be a constant source of *news* and commentary. Actually, I was counting on Malloy to do a critique of Olio d'Oliva next week. Oh well," with a quick tilt of his head and a shrug.

"You are wasting your time if I am on your suspect list," he continued. "I both enjoyed her camp and, of course, despised her ability to make or break just about anything. Perhaps I was jealous." He gives a coy turn of his head and a smile. Then he sits on the sofa with flourish, his arms outstretched along its spine. "But not enough to kill her." He raises his brows for emphasis. "Honestly, as long as my restaurants and I were regularly mentioned, I was basically a fan and will continue to be a fan of that little rag. I receive the news of her departure with ambivalence. Nonetheless, I stand in admiration of her stylish exit."

"Her stylish exit? What do you know about her manner of exit?"

"Well. Murdered." His hand moves to caress the nape of his neck. "We all die. Not all of us go out at the hand of a murderer. That is... chic, wouldn't you say, Deputy?" Turning, he looks directly at Rodriguez, winks, then back to Riley. "Lieutenant?" A broad, toothy smile spreads across his handsome face.

Riley looks into Jayden's eyes, searching, waiting a long pause before saying, "That's it for now, Mr. Listeri. Thanks for your time." The deputies leave.

Jayden walks to the large center window above Main Street.

Below, Rodriguez opens the vehicle door, sits, and says, "I don't like that guy. He's lying."

"Is that your expert opinion or a reaction to that wink?"

Rodriguez just turns his head and gives Riley a glare with his lips pursed. Then they both laugh. "Yes. I believe he is. Indeed!" she says as she drives away.

Jayden watches the deputies get in their vehicle and drive away. Then he looks out at the icy waters of the lake. He observes the hole in the storm, a patch of blue sky exiting over the eastern ridge, the next storm already moving on. He knows that this is the quiet before the monster storm. His eyes drop down to his left, to the hardwood floor beneath his feet, as he ponders Logan Malloy's rather convenient murder and the haunting stare of her cold dead eyes.

3

SOARING AND SWOOPING

Before Sheriff Jason Noble heads up the mountain, he confers with his undersheriff and his captain of investigations, a brief meet with his key staff. Then Noble heads to Moluku Lake. The snow is building on the road, but it won't slow his service vehicle.

He got the call from Sheriff Wade and Chief Billings in that order just after dawn. He assigned a bright, aspiring lieutenant with one unique qualification for this particular case.

Lieutenant Lauren Riley is an asset and a problem for Sheriff Noble. She is bright. Intuitive. Diligent and cool under pressure. She is respected by her fellows and a rising star in his office. But she is also far more than that.

She is infectious. It's that smile. And it is how ferocious she can be. And it's how she looks in her uniform... and out—not that Jason had ever seen her without clothes, but at social events, in civies, well: tall, strong, and beautiful. If he let himself ponder, he would feel things he had no business feeling, thinking.

There is one other advantage and risk, but he knows she can manage it. Besides, he is going to keep an eye on things as much as possible. He refuses to consider that maybe that is really why he assigned her to this case. Normally, he'd send up a couple of deputies. But this is exceedingly high profile. And it is something else. It is an opportunity to be around her, out of Butte County, to work together directly. He quickly tells himself it isn't about that. She is just perfect for this assignment. He dismisses any wandering train of thought.

He decides not to tackle the problem in Moluku Lake lodge directly. First, he calls Riley and Rodriguez in for a chat at the local Moluku Lake Police Department. He arrives before his deputies, so he decides to chart the way with Howard Billings, Moluku Lake's Chief of Police. "Hey, Howard. I'd say good to see you, but I don't think there is anything good about this."

"That's an understatement. Why do you think I kicked it to you? Well, that and we just don't have the resources or the experience to deal with it. Thanks for coming up."

"Yeah, well, here we go. There is no way this lands well? No way it was a simple burglary?"

"Not a thing of value seems to be missing—her money and cards seem to be untouched." Chief Howard Billings is an everyman: strong physique but a bit of mushroom just above his duty belt, tanned arms and face, thinning hair, but pleasant features and a bit of country in his style and manners. "Naw. This is someone pushed over the Malloy edge, and it's going to be a mess. I heard she finally had the goods on Oeillet."

"Just so you know, Oeillet's already put his two cents in. In my office, first thing. He was down that hill like a rocket. And he thinks Flynn did her. Thinks she had something on him."

"I'm afraid his visit was my doing, Jason. He popped in here before dawn, and I pointed him at you. Better you than me. Sorry. Logan had something on all of us."

"Well, she didn't have anything on me."

"I wouldn't be too sure. It didn't have to be true, ya know. Just dirt thick enough to stick to your britches. Good enough for her."

Jason felt a slight twisting chill in his belly for no reason. "So, what you are saying is it could have been anyone who rose to her attention."

"That is exactly what I'm saying. You don't deserve this, but at least you don't have to see the cast of characters every day like I do. By the way, Sheriff Wade in Quincy has weighed in and offers any help you need. Technically, our county would be the lead agency, but he's not equipped for this, and he doesn't want any part of it either. So no toes to worry about there. Says he'll give you any of his resources on request."

Somewhere around three layers beneath his focus, Jason is grateful he does not live in a tiny town like this. He is aware of his behavior every waking moment as it is. He says, "Do me a favor and ask him for a couple of his deputies just to cover the ground as quickly as possible. We got a lot of work to do. Nice to spread this across the agencies. I could use anyone you can spare as well."

The desk officer pokes her head into the chief's office. "Chief, there are two deputies here asking for the sheriff."

"Yeah. Mine. I want to talk to them," the sheriff explains.

"Sure. Here, use my office. Not a lot of privacy in our building."

"Actually, I want you to stay, Howard. You can add perspective. And I want them to be armed with a map of the known land mines and likely hand grenades."

The officer ducks out and is back in a flash, pointing the two deputies into the office as the chief replies, "That's only fair, Sheriff."

"Sit down, Deputy, Lieutenant. Chief Billings, this is Lieutenant Riley and her partner, Deputy Rodriguez. The chief was just saying that he is grateful to have you on this, and so am I." Sheriff smiles at both in turn, lingering on Riley just one second, held by her face, smile. He sits.

"I sure am," Billings says.

Sheriff Noble looks at his team, now seated after greetings. "I talked to the coroner on the way up. He says definitely gunshot to the heart, and time of death looks like between ten and midnight. Through and through with enough left to shatter the plate glass window. Looks like a 45. The freezing temperature slowed everything down, but they also act as a second process for time check."

Riley offers, "We talked to a number of people at the newspaper. No love lost among her colleagues—but they all seem to revere her. Weird. We have their alibis to check."

"My officers can help check on alibis."

"Any idea who at the paper benefits from this?"

"Not sure. Malloy owned the paper outright. No family we know of," Billings replies. "So it's to whom she leaves it and who can keep it going. She has an ambitious protégé, eager to wear the mantle. But apparently, it is questionable whether she can carry the water. At least, not the way Logan did."

"Guess we'll have to wait and see. That could be important," Rodriguez says.

Sheriff asks, "Can we get someone to verify who's going to head up the paper, Howard?"

Howard nods.

"Great. What about the love life?"

The chief speaks, "No love life. Logan only had conquests and useful alliances. So don't count on any love triangles or such."

"No. But maybe disappointed prospects or a discard. And maybe someone who just didn't like being a tool."

"Too bad that the readiest source of gossip just bit the dust. It would be helpful to consult with Malloy on the dirt associated with the list of suspects."

"Do we have a list?"

"Right now? What's the population of Moluku Lake?" said Riley, not meaning to be funny. They all have a chuckle, except for Riley. It's not that she doesn't see the humor; it is that she is a bit alarmed at the prospect.

"We want to go over the newspaper for the past couple of months and see who she targeted in particular," Rodriguez says.

"Could use some help with that." Noble looks at Billings. He nods again.

"We already talked to Jayden Listeri, who she skewered last weekend. No alibi."

"That's a surprise. Thought he had a different lover every night."

"Well, apparently not last night. Again, too bad. Logan could have given us the scoop."

"And as far as gossip is concerned, try Elyse James. She was Logan's right hand. If there's dirt, she's your best source now. She had the gossip column byline and probably knows a lot. Maybe more than Malloy."

"We can do that."

"So what's this bit about Malloy and Flynn?"

"Logan had her hand in everything, and so she's scratching whatever there is on the casino deal. And Flynn isn't eager for the competition for Eagle's Nest. Think about it. A big casino moving into Moluku Lake. Definitely will take some wind out of the resort's sails and maybe worse. Flynn has no license for gaming and no prospects of that ever happening. So the casino is a huge threat to his domination of the money in this town."

"So, how does that make Flynn the killer?"

"Logan Malloy made no secret that she had dirt to put Flynn in his chair and eliminate the objections to the casino."

"Surely he's not the only objection in town. And can they really stop it?"

"No. But he has the money and the clout to make trouble, slow it down to burden the financial bankroll. Anyone else just doesn't like the gambling or the Rancheria getting such an influential foothold on Moluku Lake. But they can't make the waves that Atticus Flynn can."

Lieutenant Riley gives only a split-second thought before interjecting into the conversation, "But Moluku Lake is the Maidu. It was Maidu migration grounds long before..." as her brain engaged ahead of her feelings, "...people started buying land, building cabins, and turning it into a resort." That is a much more filtered version than originally dawned in her brain. She thinks of her mother and the lore of the migrations, the lake and the hunts before the Europeans. Sheriff Noble is watching her. "There's that balance. Good catch, Lauren," he thinks.

Behind all her dander, Riley also knows that the casinos are not really the Maidu. The Rancheria's are just capitalizing on the population's propensities for vice. She did find it an interesting twist that the Maidu were gaining traction, using the corruption of the Europeans against themselves. She had grown up listening to lore about the Europeans.

Riley is half European and knows that whites are no saints but no more evil than any other race. She also knows that in

"Can she verify that?"

"Of course not. She was asleep, what do you think?"

"So you have no alibi for that time?"

"I was there! I wouldn't leave my daughter alone."

"Interesting. You did this morning."

"What?"

"You were at Malloy's house, and your daughter was at home. Alone."

"That's different. That's my routine. I go early before she awakes. She knows if she does wake up, I'll be right back. I wouldn't just leave her in the night. I didn't leave her last night!"

"Apparently, can't establish that. The snow would have covered evidence if you snuck out and went to Logan Malloy's and shot her dead."

"With what? I don't have a gun!"

"Doesn't mean you couldn't get one."

"But I didn't get one. I didn't shoot her. I found her dead."

"What did she have on you?"

"Nothing."

"Logan had something on everyone."

"I didn't rise to that level of attention. To her, I was just a tool to keep her house clean. I don't think she thought twice about me."

"And that must have been insulting and infuriating."

"I'm not stupid. Being beneath her radar was the best place to be. As long as she paid me, I didn't care. And she paid me well. Put that note in your file. She's gone, and so is the income I got from her. Add that into your thinking."

Riley stares hard into Betsy's eyes. They are clear and unflinching. Riley is certain that Betsy is not lying. But she is equally convinced that she is fiercely protecting something.

"You have no alibi. You can go, but don't go missing, or I'll put out a bulletin on you so fast, you won't know what happened."

Betsy gets up immediately. She is shaken. Again. "I'm not leaving. I have an engagement this evening. And I intend to keep it."

Betsy unlocks and gets into her car, then just sits there, her eyes indexing from left to right, darting. What was she going to do? She folds in her lower lip and gently presses her front teeth into it just a bit. Then she drives home, eager for a stiff bit of Jack to calm her. She is expecting company.

Elyse James giggled over the phone when Lieutenant Riley asked her about Jayden Listeri. "One of my favorite subjects, Logan's too, God rest her. He is just such a robust source of gossip."

"So I hear, but part of that is his equally robust social life. What are the chances he was alone last night, at his loft? Any angle that puts him in someone else's company or somewhere else?"

"Well, we don't have him under surveillance!" She was laughing. "That's your department, right? But I can tell you that he is usually somewhere doing something and rarely alone, regardless. Is he a suspect?"

Riley ignored the question and asked one of her own. "Would you tell me if you knew?"

"Perhaps. I just wouldn't tell you *how* I knew if I did. It's our sources that we guard most jealously. And I'm not inclined to keep secrets if they are juicy. Probably would have been published if there was any newsworthy alliance." Then she smiled slyly, and although Riley could not see the smile, somehow it came across the space between them fine. Elyse

James enjoys secrets, keeping them and exposing them as it suits her, when it suits her. She is an aspiring power monger. Once again, Riley knows Elyse James is also harboring something. It would be amazing if she didn't know far more than she is willing to share. Elyse adores the game and sees herself as one of the players, Riley decides.

"I can make this official, Ms. James, if that would make it easier for you."

"Why, Officer, am I a suspect?"

"Lieutenant, actually. Ms. James. Just about everyone is a suspect right now. And you suddenly have a clearer channel of incursion into your former boss' empire and license to exert your own personal power, with Logan Malloy out of your way. I see you as a genuine prospect. I like you a lot for this. Perhaps a little less coy and a little more forthcoming would be in your best interest."

A more direct response: "Think what you will. I didn't kill Logan Malloy, and this call is over."

Riley was trying to cover her bases as swiftly as possible but wished she had gone back to the newspaper for that interview. They would need to talk to James again soon.

"Come in," she says softly to the unlocked door.

He turns the knob in his hand and enters as the door gives way to his push. There isn't a lot of time. Never is. But it doesn't take a lot of time. She is ready, a light pink teddy with laces holding it together in the center and "V"ing deeply, sharply to her lower lips. Her bronze skin shines through the lacing; her breasts strain at the "strands." She is a glorious figure eight, and her arms reach out to beckon him into an embrace.

He melts into her in every way: his hands pull her in by her buttocks, and he feels her firm breasts press him such that he has to lean in to reach her open mouth. When he does, warm honey begins to flow throughout his body. Sensations surge. They are a form of pain but also intense pleasure.

He feels a small bow behind, at her waist. He pulls one of the dangling strings, and everything between him and Betsy loosens, and then the lovely brown body is utterly available. There is something erotic about being fully clothed with a naked woman in his arms. Something so jolting that it actually causes him to lean his head back for just a second, a slight roll to the side before he joins her in removing his uniform, and the real fun begins in earnest, kissing as often as he can.

She enjoys watching his face when she is naked. She likes that he cannot keep his eyes from her breasts. She loves that he wears a duty belt with weapons and handcuffs. She enjoys pushing him onto the bed, stripping the shoes, the belt, pants, and by then, the bulging underwear.

She pauses long enough to release the cuffs from the belt and tosses them on the bed. Then she smiles coyly, with her teeth gently digging into her curled lower lip. He reaches up and pulls her down onto the bed with him. She gets her own stabbing jolts: when he first sees her, the first glance of the erection, climbing on top—and on those special days, like today, as he rolls her over onto her back and cuffs her to the iron headboard. She likes aggressive play, explosive and brief. She has hair-trigger readiness and can climax before her lover; then again and again, until he does.

Passion sated for the moment, Betsy whispers softly, urgently, "We need to talk."

Riley and Rodriguez arrive at the Flynn mansion just before noon. They are greeted at the massive glass door by a tall, thin servant with silver hair. He is wearing a long black coat, gray vest, white shirt, gloves, and gray tie. His demeanor reminds Rodriguez of a military officer he served under in Afghanistan. Under the clothing is a strong and capable frame. The tall thin servant escorts them into a sitting room just inside the three-story entrance, off to the right. His voice is soft, and he does not make eye contact, then departs.

When Marie Flynn descends the staircase and enters the sitting room, it is with regal bearing. Rodriguez stands up; Riley has not taken a seat. Mrs. Flynn is an attractive middle-aged woman, dressed in elegant clothes. She is reserved with an *almost* non-existent hint of condescension.

"Good morning, how may I help you?"

It didn't sound helpful to Riley. "Well, ma'am, I'm sure you heard that Logan Malloy was murdered last night." Before Riley can continue, there is a small inhale from Mrs. Flynn, and her hand rises slightly in surprise. "You didn't know?"

"I had a good deal of correspondence to attend to this morning after breakfast. I have not yet taken in the news. Disturbing."

"What is, ma'am?"

"Murder, Officer."

"Lieutenant, ma'am. Did you know Ms. Malloy?"

"Yes. Of course I knew *of* her. I had no dealings with her myself. But my husband did, unfortunately."

"Unfortunately?"

"She was not a pleasant person. I did not envy my husband's involvement with such a distressing individual."

"And how did she distress your husband?"

"You will have to ask Mr. Flynn that question. I do not participate in my husband's business dealings."

Anticipating disdain, Lieutenant Riley said, "I have to ask, ma'am. Where were you last night between ten and midnight?"

"Here. Bedtime."

"Can anyone verify that?"

"Certainly. Servants."

"Do you have a gun, ma'am?"

"I certainly do not. Of course, Atticus has a collection under lock and key."

"Was your husband home last night?"

"I am sure you know he was out of town yesterday and did not return until last night."

"Yes, ma'am. What time did he return?"

"I do not know. I was asleep."

"You didn't hear him come in?"

"I did not. Now, if that is all, I have appointments I need to keep. Let me know if I can be of any further assistance in the future."

"Thank you, ma'am," is said as Mrs. Flynn turns and leaves the way she arrived. The servant returns and escorts them politely, efficiently to the door.

Sheriff Noble, following a hunch, left the police station almost at the same time as Chief Billings did. It is instinct that separates the great investigator from the ones who follow the book. He is waiting just down the block from an apartment building where each apartment has a street entrance, rather like a row of New York brownstones. He sips coffee he poured into a paper cup as he went out the station door. And he waits.

An hour later, coffee long gone, Howard Billings exits one of the doors, down the steps to the street and into his vehicle.

The snow continues through the crisp air. The sun is completely blocked by storm clouds now. The sheriff stiffens his lower lip with his chin muscles, pushing it up into his upper lip, and shakes his head. Then gets out and taps on Howard's window just before he pulls away.

"Let's get another cup of coffee, my friend. We need to chat."

"Howard's head fell back to the headrest and then he nodded. "Follow me to a coffee shop up the way."

Howard has a thing for Betsy that cannot be denied. Of course, he has a wife and kids, so it is complicated. Howard believes in his marriage and admires his wife. Cheryl is a good partner. She takes care of home and family and is his center of balance. But she has an ordinary figure, in her forties after three kids. Sex is as much obligation as it is pleasure—labored, for both of them. Often it is easier not to bother.

Betsy, on the other hand, is sexy and thrilling. Some men are particularly attracted to a woman with plus-size curves, especially when the woman is young and skin is firm, plump, and smooth. It can be compelling. Betsy is more than that. Beyond the immediate attraction, Betsy is kind, struggling, determined, a loving mother, and undemanding. For Howard, all of it is utterly irresistible.

"OK! I admit it," Howard defends, with an effort to keep his volume in check. "I knew I was in trouble the minute Betsy called me from Malloy's house. *That's* why *I* wanted you here. The *real* reason. I didn't want to get involved directly in this mess. Can't you see that?" Sheriff Noble calmly holds his gaze, tapping the heel of his spoon on the table. Howard finds no solace in his friends eyes. "If I have anything to do with this, I might have wanted to handle it myself, steer it in another direction... and even if I didn't, it would appear that I did, could have. But I didn't do any of that, and I didn't do this murder!"

"Did Betsy?"

"NO!" The tapping spoon is annoying.

"Then why might you need to steer it at all?"

"She called me right after calling 911 this morning after she found Malloy—and she never calls me. She was shaken up and frightened. I assured her she did the right thing by calling it in and that she should just tell the truth. You don't know Betsy. She couldn't. She wouldn't do a thing like this."

"But you might have—if you thought your secret life was about to be exposed."

"But I didn't!" His eyes fixed on Jason. "Relief! I felt relief that she was dead... am relieved that she is dead! And, yes, Malloy knew. She twisted me on more than one occasion, I admit it. Maybe I did some things I wish I hadn't. Maybe I yielded to her extortion on occasion. I was in a position to squash this or pressure that. But I swear that's all it amounted to. And I told you that she had something on everyone. I tried to tell you. OK. Maybe I didn't exactly tell you, but I called you into this so you could be objective—where I couldn't. And knew if this came out, it would look bad. It looks bad, doesn't it?"

The spoon shifted in the Sheriff's hand and he used it to stir his coffee. Set it down on the saucer. Sips. "It looks *very* bad, Howard. But not for murder. I'm not liking you for the murder of Logan Malloy. I do think you are a cop whose let himself get dirty, in your own way. Count the number of people you've hurt, and then you tell me how it looks!" The Sheriff's expression has changed.

Howard Billings looks with stupefaction into the face of Jason Noble. Seconds pass. Jason is not judging. Jason is resolutely kind and unflinching. Howard leans back, and his shoulders surrender. He drops his gaze to his lap and feels the weight of consequences settle in on him. There is no way this doesn't get out.

He thinks of the favors he did. There are a lot of people in Moluku Lake that deserve at least a kick in the ass. He thinks of his wife. She's not one of them. His kids. And then he thinks of Betsy. He thinks about Internal Affairs. He thinks about his career. And he hates Logan Malloy more than ever. He hates his friend, Sheriff Noble, a little, too, at this moment. But most of all, he hates himself.

"I need you right now, Howard. But this is not going away. We'll deal with it later. The only break I can give you is time to think this through and make choices about how you prepare to deal with it and how it comes out." Jason left Billings sitting in the booth at the coffee shop and headed to Eagle's Nest. The sheriff realizes a need to watch this one more closely than he had originally anticipated. Somehow, that makes him feel relief. And simultaneously, excited. Then he feels a gripping in his gut.

Jason is divorced. The job. He knows he handled it badly. Fortunately, no kids to make it complicated. But Jason understands that the job gets messy and disturbing. Jason's devotion to his career wore on his ex-wife. Soon their time together was cool, then cold.

Now, at times, tired, even exhausted, Jason longs for that compelling sense of turn-on, that overriding, hot, butter-melting, contorting sense of desire that could shove the stress away for at least a little while. Maybe he had been too quick to want that available, readily available: marriage. Maybe he had never considered the commitment, the other side of the equation: what it felt like to be second in line for consideration, to be an availability. He shudders inside at the greatest failing of his life so far. He worries that it is too late for him. Or maybe, he is already committed. To the job.

His mind drifts to the dark, clear eyes of Lauren Riley. He starts to fill up with longing. Then he thinks of Howard Billings.

Dating is risky, entangling, time-consuming... yet, there is appetite. The world he spends his time sorting through, the way women dress, behave, the way he wants them to behave... oooh. Images warm him. Instantaneous surges move out into his body.

He blew his marriage. Now what? He feels for Howard. He also envies him. Then he thinks about the mess Howard is in, opens the window to let in the cold air, and shoves it all from his mind.

4

FEMALES OF THE SPECIES

Up a small road into the eastern foothills above Moluku Lake, there is a geodesic dome nestled into the pine trees.

It is made with triangle shapes of wood and glass rising to an upper latitudinal circle, a ring at the top. From inside, it is like wedges of light, green, blue, or like today, the weight of snow and shards of ice—and on a clear night, galactic splendor.

It is not ostentatious. It appears to belong right where it is, as if it grew there or was dropped there: a large pinecone on the hillside. It is home to Elizabeth Skymyn Riley. Most call her Ellie Skymyn, but to some, she is known as the Kapá or the Great Bear. Kapá lives in the world of the whites but treads in the world of the Maidu. Maidu means "man" in the language of the People. It suggests that the People did not know to name themselves. They were who they were: the animal species called Maidu.

Kapá watches Roger Haawim walk up the path to her home under storm clouds that have pushed the patch of blue out of sight now. It is snowing on the eastern ridge.

"Logan Malloy was murdered last night, Kapá."

"Yes. She was cankerous, but useful."

"She will not be able to keep Flynn at bay after all."

"This will not alter our strategy. I must say, I did not figure this. But the world unfolds as it is supposed to, and there is always another option, Roger. Frankly, that wasn't the best option to begin with. "

At this point, Haawim is mounting the steps to the pinecone house, up and into the warmth of Kapá's home. The door closes as the scent of wood, herbs, and berries fill his nostrils.

"This will give that pompous Flynn a clear path to block everything."

Kapá smiles, then quietly chuckles. "No. The path is never as clear as it appears, Roger."

"What does that mean? He will stop at nothing! Malloy's extortion was the only viable way. She is dead. How will he be stopped now?"

"I was not convinced that would stop him to begin with. He is a difficult and somewhat unpredictable creature. I see him like fire in crystal, ablaze and unreachable. I placed my small wager on the probable pressure point. But, Roger, do you believe that is the only plan in my mind? Do you think that was the sum of my thinking?" Kapá observes Roger, his anxiety over that which is beyond his control. "Roger, I believe you will benefit if you can learn to channel useless emotions into useful energy to accomplish what you want. Surrender to patience when restraint is essential."

"OK, Kapá, let me in on it. I am eager for hope in this mess."

The old woman looks at the agent and smiles from way back behind her eyes. "I must ponder this a bit. I have been doing so all morning. This is more delicate."

"Do you think Flynn could have killed her?"

"Not likely. That is not at all in his character. He is cunning, not prone to something this obvious. However, whoever did this thing helped him out. Who else did it help out? Think on that one, Roger. I am." She pivots toward one of the glass wedges and looks up at the increasing fall of snow. "Roger, did you know eagles can fly through the snow? It is snowing very heavy before they do not fly or hunt."

"I suppose. So?"

"They say now that the birds of prey are what is left of the dinosaurs. They ruled the earth for millions of years, Roger. They were powerful guardians of the planet for more years than primates have existed. They are not to be trifled with or underestimated."

"I guess. But I don't see what that has to do with casinos or Atticus Flynn."

"Do you also know that the female eagle is far more ruthless than the male?"

"Are you speaking of Logan Malloy? She was ruthless. Yes." Roger Haawim watches the Great Bear as she ponders the sky and knows that when it comes to eagles or the business of their Rancheria, Kapá is ferocious and clever. "Isn't that true of bears as well, Kapá? Aren't the females always more ferocious?"

Kapá flicked her brows a bit in acknowledgment. "Indeed." Kapá smiled and her eyes narrowed. "Yes Indeed. I think that we will go to the Art Council Fundraiser at the lodge tonight, Roger."

"Of course. They expect the Council to present a donation."

"Yes. The Council has authorized a sizable donation. But I think tonight, we will deliver it in person." She spins herself around to look directly at Haawim. "Better get out your best bid and tucker."

"What does that mean?" Roger queries.

"Honestly, I don't know. But in the world of the European, it means dress in your finest."

"I guess that means my feathered headband. Don't know if it's even in one piece at this point."

"Don't be ridiculous. Wear your tux. I'll wear the feathers for both of us." Then she turns over her shoulder and gives Roger a wink, and they both laugh. "Trust the universe. Everything happens exactly as it should when it should. All is well, Roger."

"May not have that party at all if this blizzard really sets in by tonight," he says.

"Oh, they will have it. After all, it is a ski resort. Snow can't slow down action in that town. Remember, I told you. Eagles can fly through snow." Her dark eyes are twinkling.

"Sheriff Jason Noble to see Atticus Flynn."

"I am sorry, Sheriff. Mr. Flynn is not here."

"Where is he?"

"He *was* here. He had a meeting. Appointments. I don't believe he will return until this evening for the gala."

"Then I will speak to Eli Lucas."

Jason made his bones in the department as a successful criminal investigator. He feels himself being drawn into the intrigue of this case. He has a hunch.

Eli Lucas receives the news of the Butte County sheriff's arrival to talk to Atticus with considerable apprehension. The fact that the sheriff wants to talk to him is equally disconcerting since that places him in the position of figuring out what to say about something he has been pondering all morning. "I would say good morning, Sheriff, but it is not all that good, is it?"

Sheriff Noble chuckles snidely. "For someone, it is a good morning, or so it would seem. Someone wanted Logan Malloy dead, and, well, she is dead. The question is, who is that happy person?"

Eli's stomach seizes and acid rises. He thinks before answering. "If you are going to put it that way, I guess there are a number of folks that are relieved if not happy. But I am not one of them, I assure you."

"Is Atticus relieved? Happy?"

"It is possible that he is among the relieved. Yes." Eli is hammered by the images of Atticus with his Bollinger and his roses. But he remains stoic. As stoic as it is possible for him to be at this moment. Sheriff Noble reads: smokescreen.

"Did you see Atticus this morning?"

"Yes."

"Was he upset? Relieved? Anxious? ... *Happy*?"

Eli cannot contain a nervous laugh that erupts and subsides quickly. "Relieved. I'd say he was relieved. Definitely how I would characterize him this morning. But he had a busy day and had to leave shortly after arriving, so that is all I know."

"And where is he right now?"

"I do not keep Atticus's calendar. We have an executive assistant, Ms. Brody. She may know."

"Will she have a record of his travel arrangements?"

"Yes. Of course."

"Then I would like to speak to her. Why don't you take me to her so she can pull up records? I have a few questions to ask her about her boss."

Eli complies with a troubled heart, straight into the office between the two executive suites. "Ms. Brody, this is Sheriff

Jason Noble. He is here about Logan Malloy and has a few details I believe you can clear up." He smiles, gives a slight bow of his head, and steps back to listen.

His eyes give away his concern to Irene Brody, and she is quick to convey a smile. "How can I help you, Sheriff?"

"I'd like to see Flynn's itinerary for this most recent trip. And I want everything—flights, hotels, a car if he rented one, restaurants, everything. Please."

Irene's fingers move efficiently across the face of her tablet, and then she says, "Do you want me to send them to you, or do you want paper?"

"I want you to send them to this email, and, yes, give me the paper. Did Flynn change his itinerary on this trip?"

"No. Not that I know of."

"What does that mean? Did he or didn't he?"

The printer goes to work. "I can only speak for the arrangements I made, and I didn't change anything. I didn't receive notice of a change to the itinerary. However, his flight was late, and the driver didn't get him in the limo until after nine o'clock."

"How long is the drive?"

"Three plus hours in good weather. Probably at least four last night."

"We need to talk to the driver."

"Yes, sir."

"Where is he right now?"

"The driver?"

"Flynn."

"Mr. Flynn had a meeting this morning, and then he said he had appointments and would not be back until this evening."

"What appointments?"

"I would imagine personal, as I don't have anything specific on my calendar for him."

"Does he often have personal appointments that are not on your calendar for him?"

"Mr. Flynn is the owner of this resort. He comes and goes as he pleases. If he blocks out personal time, it is none of my business."

Jason remembers his own words earlier this morning: *Everyone up here is doing someone.* "*So who is Atticus Flynn doing on 'personal' time?*" he thinks to himself.

The sheriff goes to the security office and requests the video recordings from earlier in the morning. He watches Atticus arrive, go to the wine cellar, pull a Bollinger out of the chiller, go by the flower shop and give a flourish of directions. By the time he got off the elevator on the top floor, he had an entourage behind him and his carnation boutonniere, all but prancing down the hall to his office.

Jason smiles a crooked smile and shakes his head. "So he was relieved," he thinks to himself, replaying in memory, Eli squirming simultaneously with Atticus sipping champagne. He continues to review the various cameras tracking Atticus through the morning. The only place he couldn't track was when Atticus entered an elevator. At 1:42 p.m., Atticus left a conference room after a meeting with a producer and headed to an elevator. But then, Atticus Flynn disappeared.

"He can't just disappear. Is he still in the elevator? How can that happen? Where did he get out? Why is there no record in the elevator? I want to see the elevator records. That elevator took him somewhere. People don't evaporate! I want to know where that is!"

"I couldn't say, sir."

"Can't or won't? Tell me, what just happened here? If you don't, I'll take you in as a material witness and hold you until you do!"

The security guard tells Sheriff Noble, "I will probably get fired for this, but there is a private floor where there are no security cameras. Atticus Flynn took the private elevator to the private floor. It is for the highest-level guests, politicians, celebrities—people with a lot of money and influence. Sometimes they do not want to be on camera."

"Seriously?"

"We live in a world where privacy is at a premium. A premium some are willing to pay to ensure..." the guard pondered, "...for example, that the likes of Logan Malloy don't find their secrets."

"And did Logan Malloy ever get access to these premium secrets?"

"Not from me, sir."

"Then from who?"

"I am not the only shift, and I am not the only one with access to these files. I can't speak for anyone but myself. I swear!"

Outside, the wind is blowing, and the snow is thick, falling in blankets. Jason Noble stands there while the gears turn. If he could figure this out, so could someone else. A secret floor. People with secrets. Malloy with money and dirt on everyone. What had she found out?

"Put that file on a thumb drive, now. Where is this floor?"

This time, the sheriff goes directly to the office of Eli Lucas, without announcement, without introduction. "I am going to need the names of your entire security department, and I want you to escort me to the secret floor, Mr. Lucas."

Eli's eyes close for a second as he inhales. "I don't think that is a good idea. It is against our policy, and it will violate the privacy of our guests, our clients."

"I believe I may have to violate their privacy, just a bit, since that is where Atticus Flynn seems to have disappeared... on camera, or off-camera is perhaps more accurate.

"Do you have a warrant, Sheriff?"

"No. But I can get one with the video and the elevator that transports an individual into thin air!"

"I am afraid, Sheriff, without a warrant, I simply cannot and will not comply."

"I would prefer to do this with as little fuss as possible. But if you do not cooperate, I will get a warrant. In the meantime, I believe I will need to make sure everything remains exactly as it is right now. If you are buying time or obstructing our investigation, I will need to make sure that no one and nothing leaves the premises, nothing is destroyed, that sort of thing. If you prefer, I will fill this place with police and prevent anyone from leaving or entering until I get a warrant."

With the gala now just hours away, Eli swallows and calmly looks up into determined eyes. "Then Sheriff that is what you will have to do."

The sheriff picks up his radio and gives the orders, noting in his mind that the pudgy little man in front of him is tougher than he looks.

It does not take long for police cars to arrive at Eagle's Nest and deploy to all exits and elevators. By now, the snow is a problem for anyone driving. In Moluku Lake, most vehicles are prepared for this. Certainly the police. Riley and Rodriguez hear the call, grateful for their four-wheel vehicle. Nonetheless, the plows are out, clearing way for the gala traffic, so the light goes on the roof. Still, it is tricky to get to the lodge, which is already under siege. But the town is also besieged by the weather. "I bet this is going over great!" Rodriguez states.

There is no courthouse in Moluku Lake, so Jason sends an email to his office down the hill to obtain a warrant. As the sheriff does this, Eli is calling the resort attorney and thinking as fast as he can.

Eli tells Sheriff Noble, "Butte has no jurisdiction in Moluku Lake. Jason tells him that he is acting under the mutual-aid agreement, and the warrant is legal." Eli shakes his head.

Jason calls Howard on the radio. Howard is just arriving at the lodge. Together, they decide to declare a local emergency due to the storm—now a blizzard—and close the roads.

Howard calls the mayor for concurrence. That sets in motion an even greater level of cooperation and authority. And the mayor is delighted to assist them, quickly obtaining the approval of a Council quorum. The lodge is under house lockdown and right before the big night.

Eli is calculating that most of the guests are already in town. How will this impact the gala? He is urgent but calm when he reaches the resort's attorney, but there is no ground for objection. After repeated attempts to wiggle, all shot down by the attorney, Eli hangs up the phone and looks up at the sheriff. "Can we wait until our attorney arrives?" Jason shakes his head.

Eli unlocks the private elevator, and it descends to the fifth floor, just below the offices and Aigle Noir.

The two deputies deploy to knock on every door on the floor. If the door opens, the deputies apologize and do a quick check. If the door does not open, it is opened, and they check: empty. Just before 3:00 p.m., Riley knocks on 521, and no one answers. "Open it," she says to Lucas. He obeys. When the door opens, standing naked in the middle of the room is Jaden Listeri, sipping Bollinger next to a vase of roses.

When Room 523 is opened, the sitting room is empty, but Atticus Flynn is lying calmly on the bed, fully clothed, except his bow tie hangs loose, the top button of his shirt is open, and his jacket hangs on the back of a chair in the suite. Hearing the lock open, he does not bother to move until Sheriff Noble is standing inside the sitting room of the suite. Then Flynn rises from the bed, poised, unsurprised, saunters into the sitting room, does not acknowledge the sheriff's presence, calmly goes to the mirror above the fireplace, and straightens several hairs that appear to be out of place. Then he turns.

Sheriff Noble watches all this with smothered disdain. *"Damn! He is an arrogant ass,"* Jason thinks to himself. But he waits, enjoying this routine. When Atticus turns from the mirror, Jason decides he has given the "arrogant little ass" sufficient time to perform. "Do you want to explain yourself, Flynn?"

"I was patiently waiting for you to explain yourself, Sheriff. I don't need to explain anything."

At that moment, Lieutenant Riley opens the adjoining doors between the two suites and enters 523. Over her shoulder, Atticus can see Jayden Listeri zipping his trousers in the other suite.

"You are actually going to tell me that you were napping?"

"I do not feel compelled to tell you anything at all. I am in my resort, doing nothing that should draw your attention whatsoever. But I realize you are conducting a murder investigation. Therefore, I will deign to tell you that I got in early this morning from a business trip. Little sleep and I had a few glasses of bubbly to celebrate... a business triumph this morning. Went to my head. I needed to let it pass. After all, I have an event tonight, here at the resort, actually."

"What do you say if I tell you that I think you are up here involved in a relationship with Jayden Listeri, celebrating, or maybe thanking him for knocking off your business adversary, Logan Malloy? What if I tell you, I think you two got something going, and that is what Malloy had over your head, and that is why she is dead? What if I tell you that I believe I have just nabbed the two primary suspects in the Malloy murder?"

"Why, Sheriff. I have a bulletproof alibi. That's what I'd tell you."

"But Jayden does not. So I say he did it *for* you. What do you say to that?"

Jayden interrupts, "*I'd* say, prove it if you think it!"

Far Away, Long Ago, a Desperate Flight

Maurice Bouche knew he had to take desperate measures to escape the général's wrath. Bouche grabbed the rail of a passing impériale and swung himself—as only an able young man can, onto the steps that led to the upper, open deck. There he shielded himself from view as much as possible and tried to make himself invisible to the outskirts of Paris. Skillfully, he jumped off the still-moving transport ahead of notice and headed into the alleys and shadows.

He knew that he had not outdistanced the revenge that awaited him if apprehended by either the Général or any of the legions he had doubtlessly sent on Bouche's trail. He didn't give thought to the bounds of his fear. He only knew he had made an enemy, a formidable and merciless enemy. Things were chaotic, and revenge was extracted upon France and on anyone who could be portrayed as a villain in the face of a bitter defeat.

Bouche took some of the precious gold he had left and secured passage on a farmer's wagon, towering with lashed hay bales, and headed south out of Paris. He paid extra so he could leave without question or controversy. He counted on the chaos in the countryside at the end of the Franco-Prussian war to mask any other details of his departure. The journey was slow. When his stomach complained more than he could bear, he traded his pistol for enough francs to buy food on the way. He was not pleased at the loss of his pistol, but he had nothing with which to arm it. On the other hand, he was eager to spend the francs, as they were nearly worthless and devalued by the day. He would need the last of his gold before his escape was secured.

He continued south by similar means and then by sea until he made it to the port of Bastia in Corsica. There he signed on to a privately-held ship with a tattered yet lingering letter of marque, commissioned to carry all forms of hostility permissible at sea by the usages of war. This included attacking foreign vessels, the enemy, and allies and taking them as prizes, everything, from cargo to crews. It also included raiding and plundering seaports of the enemy, a designation loosely interpreted by many of the brigands who commanded such vessels. The ship sailed first west and south, then far west to the new world, where news, laws, and recension of orders would travel far slower than the trade winds.

The fringe of order, the timing, and the modus suited Bouche, but the discipline imposed by the ship's hierarchy did not. The crew were treated like slaves, and some were indentured. They were all trapped at sea under totalitarian domination and subjected to harsh routines and punishments. Bouche survived whatever way he could devise, including selling out his shipmates, deceit, and chicaneries that made the crew hate him as much or more than the captain of the ship.

By the time the ship arrived in San Francisco, the war with Prussia was long over, and France was in a civil war between fledgling socialists and what would become the newest republic. Meanwhile, the privateers, at heart opportunists, sailed on without commissions to loot and become pirates in the new world.

Once anchored off the peninsula, Bouche did not await his destiny. At first dusk, he carefully found his way aft, quietly over the edge and down the wooden fantail till he could quietly lower himself into the water. He did this one step ahead of getting his throat slit either aboard or in some back alley of the bowery by his own shipmates. Had he stayed, if no one else got him, he might have been hung for treachery by his captain.

By now, Bouche's heart was black, and his mind was ruthless. He had no country. He was twenty-three, quite alone, without recourse but to use his wits as a weapon. He saw the world comprised of those who rise up and oppress versus those who are the pawns subject to abuse. Bouche was exhausted from being a pawn, determined to become one of the oppressors.

In the city, he did not find comfort. The harbor saw ship after ship arriving: sailing vessels, steam vessels, wagons of people coming from the east. But the influx was overwhelming the port. Men were living in tents, wood shanties, wagons, or deck cabins cannibalized from abandoned ships. The word everywhere was "gold."

His plan quickly fermented and turned, like so many others, toward the riches in the hills surrounding the fertile delta. He heard talk of gold in the streams and rivers and miners pick-axing their way to a mine, a claim in the hills.

Beyond that were huge mountains. The prospects were staggering.

He also comprehended the associated treachery that had already inflicted itself upon the previously peaceful lifestyle of the Northern California valley and foothills. It was a lawless time, and that was something with which he was both familiar and comfortable. He recognized that he could have whatever his wicked heart could imagine.

He did not consider employment, and he had no investment to make. The concept of earning a thing, working for someone else, saving, inventing, building, or selling his labor or service was not in his life experience, nor did he have an appetite for it. But he did understand that desire has a price, and he did understand the effort that is compelled by wanting and taking.

5

BIRDS OF A FEATHER FLOCK TOGETHER

Elyse James enters the ballroom at Eagle's Nest, the apex of her aspirations unfolding before her eyes. She observes the crème de la crème of Northern California, parading their position and wealth. Baroque draping and faux columns give the room a palatial feel. The Council expects generous donations and therefore provides a conducive atmosphere. It is dramatic, ornate, and touched with elegance and whimsy.

There are no costumes, per se. Instead, everyone is wearing elaborate masques. But from behind this tiny bit of camouflage, the players stand out in every other way. Thoughts of the masques, Poe, and plague trickle through her mind. She files away that amusing correlation, which she will contemplate when she writes up her scoop on this evening.

She'd attended for the last several years. But she was Logan Malloy's shadow, her underling; assistant. A year ago, Elyse had her own brand-new byline, and she was learning, a faithful apprentice—a hungry student. Even so, background to Logan Malloy. Nevertheless, clever, eager, and determined, she made a place for herself at the right hand of her mentor.

Logan owned this town and loved the feel of it in her clutches. Elyse does not love it. It is a means to her ambitious ends, which she justifies in her mind as she contemplates how vulnerable they all are as they flaunt, chatter, and posture. At this moment, they are unaware of the power she now holds. Soon enough, she tells herself, consciously dampening her enthusiasm, her sense of command to keep focused. "Tonight is my coming-out gala event. Tonight, I am the *Moluku View*. The *View* is within my grasp as its brand-new editor in chief, and soon, I will have all these people in my dominion," she muses, heart pounding. "I may change the name of Logan's rag, something more explicit, maybe menacing... *Moluku Exposé*, no. *The Talon...*" Mason Oeillet catches her eye. "Oh, I like *Talon*!"

The mayor sees Elyse James even before she sees him. She is at the top of the stairs at the main ballroom door, statuesque. Tonight, she wears a royal blue gown suspended on rhinestones and lightly caressing her shape all the way to the floor. Her mask is a silver metal filigree with a delicate ribbon tie to hold it in place. Mason thinks her breasts are like thick hot candy, blobbing in a big drop about to fall.

He scrapes his gaze off of her long enough to locate his wife and make sure she is occupied. Then he makes a straight track for Elyse, glad-handing as he goes. As he approaches, he can feel everything that matters jump inside of him. She is watching his every move at the moment, which is exciting for him. Mason is wearing a vested tuxedo and a Venetian long-nose mask in bright white, contrasting his ruddy skin beneath. He does not remove it as he politely greets her, congratulates her, presses a key to a private room into the palm of her hand, and says, "Midnight, baby."

Elyse allows a tiny crank of her cheek to lift a bit of a smile, and she shakes his hand. It is not a smile of happiness. It is not even a smile of appreciation to be congratulated on something she holds dear. It is a brief and insignificant moment of gratification. She lets it pass and gracefully lets herself descend the staircase, step by step, without even a glance downward. She is finalizing her agenda for the evening, prioritizing and calculating. She has work to do.

Mason moves swiftly toward his wife and begins an earnest endeavor of being the mayor of Moluku Lake, honored guest, dutiful husband. His wife is the vice-chair of the Moluku Lake Arts Council. Vianne Oeillet sees her husband approach and greets him with a demure smile and the appropriate and respectable outreach of her hand. She is the town's first lady, the second most important person in this room, at least, in her own estimation. She is also the sister-in-law of the very most important person, Marie Flynn, chair of the Arts Council and, well, basically the empress of Moluku Lake and its culture. Mason takes her hand, smiles, and says, "Annie," giving her a peck on the cheek accompanied by some soft "Oh's" and "Aws" from those immediately surrounding them.

It is customary in this crowd to endorse marriage, especially marriages that can be measured in decades. Nouveau riche are all about change; they themselves disrupters, per se. Vieux riche, generational wealth, and position, in contrast, prefer predictable, advantageous, substantial, and secure coupling. Adulterations of those precepts should be discrete, obscured, or at least well-camouflaged.

Vianne has the resources to buy the best and address any flaw in her aging process she finds discouraging. She is shapely in a round style, a little taller than average, so she can carry it off successfully. She wears clothes that expose cleavage, show off her small waist, and flatter her round bottom. Tonight, she is in tanning bed glow, bright white, and diamonds, lots of diamonds. Her mask is an intricate design of diamanté, with a small crown at her forehead just above her nose. She feels regal, good. Amid her contentment, she keeps an eye out for her sister-in-law, running late. She is not surprised. Atticus always has to have his entrance.

Across the room, through the glass doors that open to the Eagle's Nest's steaming pools and spa, five individuals enter, obviously directly from the parking garage. Four men in impressive tuxedos, the gentlemen's dress code of this affair, and one woman, short but imposing. She is dressed in a Maidu beaded dress, leather boots, and a cape decorated in the distinctive brown-and-white eagle feathers. There is an almost imperceptible gasp, then a hush for a split second. Then the din of the crowd resumes without further ado.

Kapá wears no mask. She pauses just inside the doors and surveys the room. There is a small ensemble playing jazz in the corner on the small round stage above the dance floor. The music does not fit the décor, but then, who would dance to Bach or Rameau... the harpsichord? Inside, Kapá chuckles as she observes the flamboyant surroundings. "*At least the band is subtle,*" she thinks to herself. They do not interrupt the conversing assembly at all. Tables festooned in lordly chateau chic surround the dance floor. Kapá smiles. "*Gauche. But then, what did I expect?*"

She knows the room is surprised to see her. She always receives an invitation to any important event in Moluku Lake: she, on behalf of the Tribal Council. Usually, the Tribe just sends a check in advance that is gratefully received and announced at the event. She did not RSVP: rude. No time. But she doesn't plan to impose that much. And she wants the surprise factor. Besides, the Council has been generous to Moluku Lake—to its schools, social programs, and the arts. Kapá believes her arrival will be nothing more than a bit of welcome entertainment, perhaps a little silage for gossip.

Based on initial scoping, she finalizes plans for the evening's attendance. She smiles to see them all there, entertaining themselves with themselves, thinly disguised, adorned in their masks. Kapá is aware that Butte County is involved in the murder investigation. For a brief moment, she wonders if she will see her daughter tonight. Probably not. She makes a rough map of the "encampments" across the room and sets out. She has work to do.

As Kapá makes her way through the growing crowd of notables, small groups conversing clear the path for her, Roger, and their three escorts—sons of Maidu councilmembers. The young men are in Armani, and each has on an unadorned, sleek, silver sash, masks tied neatly behind their heads, hanging down their black hair but not touching their collars. They are bold in their simplicity and have been invited to enhance their understanding of how the world works and to lend critical mass to Kapá's presence. They are clean-cut, bright, and handsome. She enjoys how they are received without giving much regard to how she is received.

Kapá often records "reception" responses in the community. She perceives it to be a mix of disdain, respect, guilt, and a tiny twinge of anticipation—never sure exactly what a member of the Council might do or say. The ratio varies from group to group, occasion to occasion. And one more thing, sometimes a dose of envy. That one she often ponders. "Why envy?" The natives of the Northwest have suffered significantly at the hands of the Spaniards, the Mexicans, the greedy, the Americans, and their government. "Is it that they envy the strength and will of the People to endure? Do they wonder if they would have endured? Do they wonder if they will endure? Or is it the wealth and influence of the emerging Rancheria's?"

Kapá scans the room, noticing that there are several Moluku Lake PD present. Not unusual when you consider all who are in attendance here. Her attention is drawn to the double doors at the top of the staircase as they open simultaneously and are held open by two gentlemen in cutaway coats and face-fitting black masks. Through this sweep of pomp steps a couple.

Atticus Flynn is radiant in a perfect black vested tuxedo; a tiny gold thread runs almost imperceptibly in the vest. Crisp white shirt, thin immaculate black tie, his usual rings of gold and diamonds, but no other adornment. It is the perfect understatement to set off his black-and-gold beasty wolf masque, framed in sharp contrast by his silver hair. He is stunning for his sheer simplicity and exquisite execution.

On his right arm, of course, is Mrs. Flynn. Marie is just as elegant: black velvet gown, from the neck to the crest of the breast, a fine silk mesh, and around her neck, a crusted pearl necklace gleams against the black. Her masque is *un baton noir* and made in the shape of a butterfly. The wings have hints of mother of pearl for color, but the dominant markings of the butterfly are in pearl, both white and black. But something is quite different. The casual observer might not notice. But Kapá does.

Atticus turns majestically toward Marie and extends his hand, into which she places hers. All watch as they descend to applause, together in unison, graceful, practiced, and comfortable with attention. They stroll across the space that clears before them, smiling, nodding as if choreographed to a seemingly appointed spot, where Atticus turns to Marie, feigns a kiss on her hand, nods, turns, and moves away in a new direction.

Marie is immediately surrounded by the Arts Council and those eager to fawn over her. This is her night. This is the annual gala over which she presides. Her masque, suspended on the baton, is moved to and from her face, providing control as to when her face can be seen and when she wishes it covered. Her features are perfectly placed, neo-classic, porcelain, and her eyes like blue glaciers. Her expression is calm, polite. When you think she is smiling, she is actually parting her lips in a way that implies a smile, but she never shows her teeth or overtasks her cheek muscles.

Atticus is greeted by Eli with a red devil mask and Jayden with an ornate filigree half-mask covering the left side of his face, assuring Atticus that all matters of the evening are well within operational parameters.

Atticus can see Ellie Skymyn moving toward him over Eli's shoulder and does not make a pretense of leaving. Rather, he stands his ground. Eli returns to the side of Grace in her red feather mask and form-clinging mermaid dress, also red, all of which matches Eli's devil mask.

"Well, Ms. Skymyn, how delightful to see you here tonight, and what a remarkable gown. Make it yourself, or is it handed down?" Atticus said with his best fabricated smile.

"Atticus." Kapá's smile is more genuine, if restrained, and she ignores the insult. "I believe the ravens are having a good caw at the fortunes of the past few days."

"I'm sure I don't know what that means, Ellie, but if you mean they are laughing at you, then I would have to agree." Now he smiles, and it is very genuine.

"Did you kill her?"

"Don't be ridiculous."

"No. It never actually occurred to me that you did. Not your style at all. But I was compelled to ask, eager for your reaction. Nice dodge, though. And I think you should be leery."

"Which arrow did I dodge... and leery of what?"

"Logan and devils you don't yet know."

"Is that a threat?"

"Absolutely not. It is a warning, more like a prediction. This is not over for you. I'd be asking myself where it will come next and what can be done to defend against the unknown. You have many grubs, larvae, bugs, and other crawly things that may be discovered by any rock being turned. And the earth is moving."

"I'm afraid that, although you're as visual and coarse as ever," he condescends and rolls his eyes, "it is the wishful threat of someone who laid down her three aces against a full house. You've lost. Your attendance here tonight is evidence of the impact. You've either come to meet with someone to hatch a recovery plot, or you've come to wield influence to offset the loss whichever, it doesn't matter to me. I take it as a concession, and I am delighted!" Now he is grinning.

He takes her hand, lets it go, turns, and departs smoothly to Kapá's whispered parting remark, "You seem shorter this evening, Flynn. Someone cut you down to size?" Flynn is not grinning anymore.

Illustrious as Mr. Flynn is, he is more than happy to meld into the crowd and allow Marie her reign. He has a limited desire to speak to anyone tonight. He is tired, and he is now agitated. He makes his way to Eli and Grace. "Grace. No one will miss you this evening."

Grace is polite but has no use for her husband's partner. "Jealous?"

"Not at all, my dear. Believe me, not at all." He does not allow his eyes to contact Grace's. He finds her vulgar and obvious but perceptive. He does not want to see into the window of her soul. And perhaps, even more potent, he does not want her to see into his. He knows she would be glad to see the Flynns fall from their thrones. "Eli, I am sure you can handle this evening?"

Grace notices that Atticus is not quite himself, not as smooth in motion as in snapshot. She wonders what it is that puts him in discomfort—even if it is such a tiny tinge. She has rarely seen such a thing.

"Yes. Are you leaving?"

"I won't be far. I prefer to drink in private tonight!" Atticus lifts his chin in the direction of Jayden, and his eyes move toward the side door through the crowd and back. It is subtle, almost imperceptible. He could be adjusting the fit of his collar. His edge is softening a bit as he glides in the crowd, distracted.

Atticus takes his time, doing what he does so effortlessly— making people think he actually is present in the moment. In a conversation, then another. Expertly voicing small talk, making eye contact, shaking hands, removing his mask, a kiss on this cheek or that. Joking, laughing and making polite inquiries exactly as if he cares what any of them have to say or do. He is making himself warming, felt like a hearth on a cold night. Going through the motions of the great and gracious celebrity, greeting his guests, customers, his fans, all adoring followers. Then, when no one notices, like an ember of a great flame, he fades from the event.

Eli watches him go and continues to worry. He respects his partner, but within that respect is also a considerable measure of reverence for his capacity to behave selfishly, think outrageously, and have little regard for anyone else. Anyone except Marie.

Atticus openly defers to Marie in many things, except the business. At Christmas, Atticus always conspicuously goes to the jewelry store, conveniently across the highway from the lodge, to pick up Mrs. Flynn's gift, and it is always a whopper.

Eli is also aware that Atticus has a secret life, one that Eli guards zealously.

It used to be restricted. Now it is perilously close and precarious. As he watches Jayden meet up with Atticus at the side door, Eli is calculating the impact of that life hitting the headlines of the *Moluku View*. People who play with fire get burned. People who are fire burn those around them.

Kapá's first task completed, she next heads for the tall, lovely Elyse James. Elyse sees her coming, and she, too, stands her ground. "Ellie Skymyn is formidable, but so am I," Elyse bolsters herself. And to be assertive, Elyse stretches out her hand. "Hello, Ellie, my name is—"

"Elyse James, the understudy now the editor of *Moluku View*. I know who you are. Congratulations? Appropriate?"

"Thank you. Yes. Although I have big shoes to fill, I think I am ready."

Ellie sees the arrogance of youth. "Shoes. Yes. Boots, even. I hope you are, Miss James. You are young. Logan Malloy was accomplished at many things, but perhaps mostly, she was adept at playing with fire and not getting burned. Singed often. A few scars, yes. But never burned." Kapá pauses, then chuckles. "OK. In the end, it appears she got barbequed." Everyone who hears surrenders to a good chuckle. Kapá has never been known for her eloquence. She has to work at restraint, too, sometimes. "But she did what she did for years. You will find she made it look easier than it is. I wish you good luck."

Elyse nods, her chuckle settling in a broad smile at Kapá's retraction. "So true. But I am not *that* young, I assure you. And I tended those fires, stoked some of them and banked others. I think I have my own talent in the art of arson. But I thank you for your good wishes. Perhaps we should talk. I may be able to stir the ashes of your campfire. Perhaps I can turn it back into a bonfire." Elyse looks deep into Kapá's eyes and tries to convey that she has some serious fuel to offer. Explosions actually, in exchange, of course, for help when needed. She presses her thoughts forward toward this influential Maidu Councilmember.

Kapá reads it as an amateurish attempt at self-importance. And yet interesting. *"What does she think she knows? Something useful? Something new—a spark?"* Tired of the metaphor, Kapá just says, "Perhaps we will talk later," nods, and walks away. If the young Elyse has a firestick, can she manage to keep from setting herself on fire? Subtlety does not seem to be in her repertoire just yet. She hears herself perpetuate the metaphor, rolls her eyes, shakes her head, and shrugs.

She passes Eli and Grace on her path and deliberately takes Eli's hand, pivoting as she does, in order to look slightly past his shoulder and see who it is that Elyse James heads for next. She is further stimulated to see that it is to stand in line to greet none other than the regal Mrs. Flynn. Curious. Then she smiles again. "Curiouser and curiouser."

Kapá pauses to converse with Eli, who says, "I will be glad when this contention ends and we can all work to make our community strong and prosperous together."

Grace interjects, "Fat chance, honey. No one but you actually believes that will ever happen." She gently laughs, looking at the councilwoman. Grace finds her husband sweet and naïve. It embarrasses her when he tries to be political because he is lacking in any predatory instincts. Grace knows that is what Atticus does for the partnership, and she is grateful for it.

Atticus is the sort of individual who provokes adoration or disdain. Those who do not know him adore him. Look up to him, want to be him. Women are drawn to his charm and wealth. Those who do know him do not trust him and know that he is a superb user. Nonetheless, they ally with him because he always wins. For such a little man, his mass and influence are greater than the sum of his parts.

Kapá observes this exchange and recognizes that Eli, unlike his partner, seeks peace and the status quo. She reads him as a man who exists in a comfortable and contented bubble. His aspirations are for status quo. And she knows that no matter what, dramatic change is on the horizon for Eli. She also recognizes that his wife will do all she can to keep Eli steady through it all. She is more cunning than her husband. Ellie is polite, compassionate, and brief. Then she raises her chin in a gesture to Mason Oeillet, who abruptly disengages himself from the reception line and moves to greet the councilwoman with deference. "Ellie! What a surprise to see you, and what a pleasure." Then, almost a whisper, discretely, "Did you do this?"

Kapá smiles and moves the small group to a more guarded location in which to have a conversation as the young men move to form a subtle shield around them. "Seriously, Mason? Of course not. You know as well as I do Malloy was part of our plan—your plan." Kapá leans in with her eyes alight. "Although it is just delicious, isn't it?"

"No, it is not! Now how do we shut that jerk up?"

"Frankly, Mason that is your job. It is what you promised and are obligated to take care of, and I thought you had taken care of it. Now? Not exactly clear what it is you plan to do to fix this. But you will fix it, Mayor! Or you will find instead of allies, you have debt collectors back at your door."

"Yeah, I get it. But it isn't my fault." Mason tries to contain his 'huff.' "My recovery plan is simple. Flynn has to have done this. Who else has so much to gain by eliminating that witch? Once he is arrested, that solves our problem."

"I hear he has an iron-clad alibi."

"Flynn would never do it himself. He got someone to do it for him. Has to be!"

Kapá purses her lips a bit. She never has been comfortable with declarations, threats, or arrogance. It usually precedes rather grand mistakes. "We'll see. What if you're wrong about that?" She places that query deep into Mason's eyes, nods, excuses herself, and moves away, leaving him to ponder. She notices a lovely voice coming from the ensemble. Nice, but it doesn't fit in with the pretense of the evening either.

In the back of the ballroom, Chief Howard Billings pauses his rounds. He told Sheriff Noble that he would keep a low-profile eye on the charity event. Just in case. He assigned two of his officers, and he is here himself. At this moment, his attention is focused on Betsy, who is wearing a mint-green satin cocktail dress, contrasting her gorgeous brown skin, with her hair tight to her scalp. Her mask is gold, simple. He doesn't pay any attention to the fact that all the men in the room are compelled to look at her as well. He is aware that she has that effect whenever she is singing. Right now, he does not care about anything besides getting next to her again as soon as possible.

Seeds In Winter

Aboard ship, Bouche had learned Portuguese, Spanish, and English to survive and then connive. The crew included a broad cast of characters, some of them abducted, also criminals and traitors from the Mediterranean and South

America. He knew that the général's rage would endure, smoldering until something reignited it, and his arms were long. He decided he needed to lose himself in this new world and its lawless culture. "Dans le chaos, il ya des possibilités."

Bouche began with petty crime just to subsist in the beginning. Once he found his way to the foothills, he raided the lone or small miners' encampments, isolated and easy prey. Encountering them on the way with their quarry, they were vulnerable also. He managed to get his traction. Bouche traveled upstream into the mountains. There he discovered engineers and the beginnings of rechanneling the river. He found work—an exceptional choice for him. He recognized that these men were not simple miners. They had a vision of commandeering this river that ran wild through the Sierra Nevada. He wanted to learn. He worked there for six months, mostly with his ears, picking up everything he could about this extraordinary canyon and how it would play a role in the final decade of the gold rush and beyond.

One thing he learned was that on Thursday night, the payroll was brought into the camp for the workers on Friday. It arrived on a large wagon, pulled by powerful mule teams, perilously up the canyon, usually carrying equipment and supplies to the site as well.

At a natural bend in the river, where the arc was sufficiently severe, the engineers had directed workers to use great flat plows with scooping edges, pulled by mules, gouging a channel toward the hillside on the inside of the arc of the bend. When the channel was lower than the river, they laid in dynamite on the outside of the arc and dropped tons of rock onto the river, forcing it to dam and spill out into the channel. The water then did more digging and grew the new channel to carry the river.

As the old channel emptied below the rock fall, the old riverbed was exposed, and a new way of mining was available. This was a growing endeavor. Now, with the initial diversion, more workers were hired to build a diversion dam and mine the original riverbed. He comprehended their plan and the wealth it would create. The workers who would labor at it would make money, too. Money would flow out of this canyon, heading toward San Francisco. Avarice burned, and his own plans began to formulate. He would put himself between the river and the city.

When the wagon rolled into camp on a particularly wet Thursday afternoon, the wheels of the wagon were making their own channels in the mud. It had been a problem the last mile of the journey. The whackers were exhausted, trail washing out, wagon getting stuck; it was a bigger problem once the wagon stopped and settled in the work camp. A great wheel, anticipated to pull barges across the river beneath the dam, had been loaded onto the wagon. Now its weight was sinking the wagon in the downpour. The large, strong mules were creating their own set of problems. Mules are hard to rattle. But once unnerved, especially when hungry, they are stubbornly problematic—equal to their worth and reliability as engines for heavy loads on tight mountain trails.

The workers were rallied to unload the wheel. Men groaned, fell; there were injuries, chains deployed, and chaos and desperation ensued. Six men wrangled the mules, grabbing the hames, pulling amid the sloshing and the complaining whinnies and the huffs. "Get wood, give them footing!" "No rocks!"

Everyone was doing something. Men sent there, coming here, grabbing, dragging, and shouting. One grabbed a flat saddle, belts, and a harness and wrangled a rested mule from the corral. Others were dragging timber to the wagon when the wagon shifted and the wheel slid, tipping the wagon into a precarious list to the right. Now there was a scramble to get out of the path of the unsecured load, mules trapped and frantic, ropes to lash the weight. More shouting, frantic activity, men wet to the skin and covered in mud, cold, numb, and too many giving orders to bring any order at all.

No one noticed that the payroll case was unguarded, disregarded in the struggle. No one noticed when it went missing from the bull whacker's box. Well, almost no one. Bouche lashed the case to the rear housing of the saddle with a billet strap and led the mule on a path that drew no suspicion and, more importantly, no attention. Once out of the range of focus, he mounted the mule and began his escape.

The mule was not fast, but it was sure-footed, and Bouche knew that if he could keep her moving in the right direction, there would be no worry of misstep. Up on the hillside, he dared to pause, looking back at the scene below. The situation was even more deteriorated: the wheel was almost in the mud along with the wagon. He breathed to calm himself. He felt no guilt for abandoning the crisis and did not notice that he was followed.

Maurice Bouche had a vision. The engineers and miners would brave danger, work hard, and take risks, and he would wait for them to bring their fortunes to him—give their fortunes to him! He didn't stop until late in the night, putting as much distance as he could between him and the great bend in the river. When he was exhausted, he found a grove of gray pine and oak trees. It meant he was halfway down the mountain, and it gave him cover. He secured his mule, took off the case, and fell asleep on top of it.

He heard a sound and sprang up as he was attacked by two shadows. There was no moonlight, and he was weary but as ruthless as his attackers were formidable. His youth and strength were his assets, but one of the attackers had a bowie knife that glinted in the almost nonexistent light. Bouche went right for it, willing to risk anything to get it away, and when he did, he sunk it through the ribs and caught the lower chambers of the heart at his first opportunity. The opponent fell to the ground, sputtering, clutching. Bouche retained the fearsome blade in his hand but had no time to consider the fallen. One shadow remained.

The two squared off in the dark as the dying lump on the ground groaned its last. Bouche could see that his adversary was small but bullish in his build. Bouche laughed, and the grin spread across his face, baring all his teeth. He relished danger, and now, fully awake, he prepared for a fight to the death, winner takes all. He finished his laugh. "Will you take this case? Will you buy whiskey, women? For how long? I could value help, and we will use this money. Not to buy tomorrow but the next decade. Want in? Or do you want to die groaning here in the dark and cold?" He looked through the dark to see fire and cunning shining back from black eyes.

6

SPONTANEOUS COMBUSTION

At midnight, Elyse opens Room 533 and finds a drunk and eager Mason Oeillet half undressed, waiting for her with champagne and the remains of a roasted chicken he is devouring. "Hungry? I sure am, and not just for this hen!" He repulses her with his greasy hands and mouth, his pale skin stretched over a great belly.

"You can clean up before you touch me." She empties her hands of her bag and the key. He always repulses her. But up until now, keeping him pleased has been part of her plan. Tonight, she knows that will change.

"Sure, baby. What an event. They've closed the highway due to the blizzard, so everyone is here, somewhere, tonight! Good for the town. Busy tonight. Probably all crashin', eatin'— if you know what I mean—up to no good. All of it good for Moluku!" Fat Mason laughs.

"Well, who is ever up to good, really?" she says resolutely, accepting that everyone is working their angle, some more successfully than others. She says it with a hook, a provocative tone.

"Yeah, well, I want to talk about that, but first…" He comes out of the bathroom with a towel in his hands and a sordid grin on his face.

"Yeah, well, I want to talk to you first," she says half mockingly, and she drops the rhinestone straps that held the wisp of a dress in place all night to reveal the naked body everyone admired all evening. She remains up on her stilettos. With her height and the heels, she is now quite a bit taller than Oeillet. She leaves her mask in place and peers out of it with satisfaction while she steps gracefully out of the puddled dress on the floor. Mason takes in air sharply as his glands and muscles respond. He reaches to pull her into his naked torso, but she stiff-arms his attempt. "By the way, I'm changing the priorities at the paper."

"Yeah, so?" he mocks back and is moving in against her resistance, ready to ignore whatever she is about to say, oblivious as to the breadth of her intent. Elyse is acutely aware of how her body affects Mason, any man. She is counting on it.

"I've killed your hot little story, and I am going to run a series of stories. A series I'm working on. Not the one Logan was going to publish. I'm not really interested in the story on that queen Atticus Flynn. Who cares about that? Really."

She has his attention now. "A lot of people care about that story! There are a lot of people who want to see that pompous ass exposed for the fake he is. A lot of people! It has to run, and soon. The uglier, the better."

"You mean *you* want it to run. Probably those Indians want it. But there are others not so enthusiastic. I would bet that this lodge doesn't want it. *Mrs.* Flynn doesn't want it to run. Besides, I have a better story, retro, history. About corruption, murder, and deceit. Goes all the way to 1850. I'm going to run a series, you know, everyone getting up every morning to read the latest installment. It's like a true-crime kinda thing, full of gritty details. Involves the capital, and it has long legs. Worth real money."

"Yeah, right, no one cares about history, baby. And you're right about that fag. Marie won't like it, but she'll understand, it's business. Besides, my sister could use a takedown, uppity snob that she is. Just get back on track and follow through with the plan." He's smiling, shaking his head. "Stop foolin' around before you even get the feel of the thing. Now, you, baby, have the kinda' long legs I'm interested in, and I want them wrapped around me, now."

"I'll admit, watching Marie Flynn squirm would be delightful. And believe me, I'll get to her." Elyse moves across the room, looking up and imagining that smug, arrogant woman facing her society friends if the story on that faggot breaks. She shrugs and gives a tiny chuckle. "But that can wait. This comes first, and it is in *my* best interest for my series to run. Trust me, Marie won't like this one either. But then you, you really won't like it one bit, darling." She is toying, baiting, and having a ball doing it.

He is torn. He *needs* that story to run, and he wants Elyse. What game is she playing at? "*What could she mean, 'I really won't like it'?*" he barely thinks. Then he says, "That story was all worked out with Logan. She's gone. That is unexpected. But all you have to do is run it, and you will get your share of the action on this. So what's the problem? And what do you mean I won't like it?" Her fending him off is becoming annoying. Her naked strutting and assuming is infuriating.

"Well, there's my share of the action, and then there is my share of something much more considerable. Actually, it was Logan who found it. If she'd have lived, she intended to run it. But she'd dead. I'm the one driving the bus now. I think of it as her parting gift to me. I think she intended to tell me all about it last night. She invited me over for a late meet. I think she was going to let me in on it and the action. We were *very* good friends, if you know what I mean." She turns her head and smiles in a coy but sly fashion.

Mason knows exactly what she means. He half imagines the two of them together and half feels like a cat in a cage with two vipers. Why hadn't he seen that one? He begins to realize the gravity of Elyse's commitment. He underestimated that.

"And as it turns out, I'm in need of capital, and I'm going to get it. You're going to give it to me."

"You don't say." He relaxes a bit. He knows this game. "Sure. Whatever you want. Just name it."

"I want fifty million dollars. Now. You have forty-eight hours." He tenses again. "You can get it. I want it. Then I will release your exposé on Atticus Flynn, Jayden, and all the 'boys in the band. I'll delay my story... for now."

Mason pauses, exhales then lets out a belly laugh. "You're overreaching, baby. The pie ain't that big."

"No, but this pie is!" She extracts a folded set of papers from her bag and flings it at him with a snap—she held that move in reserve for quite some time. She wants him to hold it in hard copy, in his hands when he reads it. Real. Tangible. It especially gives her a thrill to be playing her ace while flaunting her naked body in front of this grotesque swine. She put up with a lot to get to this point, "but we all make sacrifices," she told herself. Now she is in the driver's seat, and she grows smug as Oeillet scans Logan's summary on the page. His brow furrows.

As he reads, she reclines on the bed. He flips through the backup material. His face tightens with sudden awareness, then fear, then rage, and then with the skill of a politician, he pulls a placid screen down, and his face goes to cardboard. The flush dissipates, corked, and back behind that, what cannot be seen is a complicated albeit faulty calculation.

"Who do you think you're playing with here, Elyse?"

"A big, rich, fancy family who runs this state and does so behind the scenes, with corruption and deceit, believing no one knows how it all started and who they really are. And, Mason, darling, I bet under the scrutiny of today's media, it will become crystal clear that the old tactics of extortion, blackmail, and treachery have not changed one bit from the old days. I bet there's more than one official, maybe even a governor that succumbed to the modern-day Black Carnation! Whattaya think?"

She watches his eyes grow large and hot. She waits for it all to settle. When it does settle, it is squinty and cold, calm. He takes a step toward her. Stops. "You think this is about me? Marie? You are a little fool!"

She is confident of her control over the power monger before her. He is not a fighter. He is an ambusher, a conniver. She sees him as helpless as he always has been—usually behind her, thrusting, his favorite position. She knows that this is about his family, and that is where the real money resides. However, Elyse has made several mistakes. For example, she has no idea what sheath protects it.

"You were using me. All this time? To get information?" He is adding up everything she said.

"Of course I was using you! You were using Logan. I was using you. It is the way of things, is it not?"

"I took care of you."

"You helped me maneuver. That's all. And now I have open waters ahead."

It is coming together in his brain. "You killed Logan?"

"No. But as it turns out, I know who did."

"Who?"

"That is for me to know... for now. But I'd be worried about that, too, if I were you."

"What the—"

"When this case blows open, you will find that it fits better into my plan than into yours. Just think about it. No matter how well you dress up a murderous bully, well, evil is still evil."

"My family is not evil, bitch. We have power and influence that we struggled to acquire. Men like my great-grandfather made this state. You have no idea what you are doing."

"And as for using you, Mason, I understand you succumbing to that throb in your pants and behaving like an idiot. But I find it sad that you thought I was actually interested in you or needed you to take care of me. After all, you are too old, too short, fat, and you have man tits! Why would someone like me actually 'want' you?"

"You bitch! You little snake! Who the hell do you think you are?"

Elyse is smiling, looking down her face in disdain. "Well, let's see, I'm the bitch that has your gonads, and your uncle's gonads, firmly in my grip. I was learning from her and using you. So what?"

"Logan Malloy was a master at this game and knew how to play. You, my dear, will find that what you have is worthless, and you have a lot to learn about the game. A little drunk on what you perceive to be power, baby? Be veeery, veery careful."

Elyse arches her back and presses her teardrop breasts into the thick air between them. Her mouth open, her tongue touching the tip of her incisor. He is seething. He cannot contain the red flush crowding his cheeks. She reads it and takes pleasure in it. She exacerbates it by touching her erect nipples and letting him see how she knows it affects him, grips him, there.

Mason knows everything is unraveled by this gorgeous, venomous reptile. Far more than he is willing to concede in front of her—and far more than she actually understands. He is suffering in his rigid container: rage, hunger, and fear. He ponders the timing. He estimates the response of others— suddenly involved, others who will not take this well at all. This is like a feather pillow with a tiny rip. Better contain it before it opens wider. Snake! In just seconds, he sees her differently. Vicious, foolish, yet... surges, panic, lust, and anger all wadded up.

Elyse observes a reaction she does not expect. A small sneer forms on Mason Oeillet's face, opening his nostrils, focusing his dark eyes. She is recalculating, but not quickly enough before he moves. "You like to learn. Let me instruct you one more time." He lunges for her and snatches her hair as she abruptly turns to cross the bed away from him.

"You wouldn't dare!"

He does not reply. He slaps her stunned face, sending her delicate mask sailing, scratching her face, caught by a tuft of hair in the knot; she cries out. He lifts her weight and throws her back on the bed, slaps her again, harder. And again. Stunned and beyond panic. He takes advantage of her availability one last time. It is not nice. It is as much about punishment, emotional eruption, as it is about physical function. She has nothing but her nails, teeth, and high heels, one lost as she kicks. She is scratching, biting at nothing. As he liberates himself, he has his hands on her throat. She has her hands on his hands, clawing. She is shocked, frantic. He is resolved. It occurs to Elyse too late that she should let go of his hands and scratch his eyes. She is transfixed, gasping powerlessly, face horrifically reddening, eyes bulging with petechiae. Then suddenly subdued, compliant, limp. His rage is ebbing, but still, he squeezes. He is exhausted, spent, heaving for oxygen, and collapses.

Vianne is handed the sheet of paper with the preliminary tally of receipts from the event. Her mask is set aside. It is late. "We did very well." She smiles as she hands it to Marie. Marie Flynn is sitting erect, quite stately, on the sofa with her feet up, legs stretched out, pearl mask upside down on the floor, leaning against the sofa with its baton, her velvet high heels neatly on the floor next to it. Marie takes the sheet and looks at the total.

Vianne looks at her sister-in-law. Marie is as relaxed as she ever allows, which is not very. There is something about Marie tonight. "You wore heels tonight. Odd," Vianne comments.

"Not odd."

"You never wear heels." Marie does not react. Vianne continues, "That's the problem with marrying someone short." A bit of a goad at Marie, who has absolutely everything, but Atticus is only five foot six. The same height as Marie. Vianne has always assumed Marie did not wear heels to prevent her from appearing taller than her husband, her elegant escort; then Vianne has a thought and says in her mind, "*Arm candy.*" She smothers a laugh. But tonight, four-inch heels. Interesting. She is not young. Her feet must be killing her.

Marie barely looks up from the sheet to acknowledge the small insult, but Vianne is not looking at her, so Marie flicks her eyebrows quickly and decides to ignore it. After all, Vianne is married to her brother—and aside from being part of one of the most influential families in the state and Marie's brother, Mason is no prize.

He is rich, powerful, and connected. He is greedy and obnoxious on so many levels. Marie shudders at the thought of Mason. More importantly, he lacks Marie's subtlety and cunning. Marie does not like Mason. But what she does like is her own ability to wield power and influence, quietly, effectively, and keep it separate from her brother's brazen wallowing and mongering.

She wants to wag her head in disgust, but that is beneath her. So she doesn't take anything from Vianne's remarks other than awareness of Vianne's envy and thinly-veiled resentment. She knows Vianne desires to elevate her own position in Moluku Lake, or anywhere else. But this is where Mason is the mayor. This is where Vianne's base is, so Vianne must content herself with being the "first lady of Moluku Lake"—first behind Marie in terms of real influence and respect. She recognizes that Vianne is expressing her own disappointments and frustration. Marie tolerates in amused silence.

"Did Atticus go home?"

"Not likely."

"Mason left. I think I'll head out unless there is anything else you need me to do."

"I have the limo and driver. I'm sure Atticus will drive his car home—if he can and hasn't already, or he'll stay here. Shall I give you a lift?"

Vianne was quick to say, "Thank you, no. I'll be fine."

"Then, good night, Annie. Perhaps I'll see you tomorrow."

"Today. It is already tomorrow, Marie." And she leaves. But she doesn't go home.

Marie is still. She does not move, slump, or slouch. She sits as she is, secure, patient, stalwart in her lifelong, everyday mask. Her mind is elsewhere. The sheet of paper heralding their financial triumph of the evening lays on her lap. Her hands lay calmly, neatly in her lap on top of the sheet. She is looking at the wall opposite her. It is an old photograph, enlarged, framed, the wild and crashing Middle Fork of the Feather River in the canyon to the west of Moluku Lake.

Empire of Mud and Ice

Maurice Bouche's stolen payroll meant he could afford to buy a saloon. There he sold whiskey and women and sponsored backroom games of any sort that would draw the lucky and, far more often, the unlucky. He wined and dined many fools until they had left with him all they could afford, salvage, beg, or worse. All of this was a front for his special corrupt world and his growing fortune. He parleyed everything into expanding his realm and sphere of influence.

He sold protection, blackmailed, and set up brothels, which he peopled with unfortunate women. Some of them were Native Americans displaced from their lands, separated from their families as the European population applied ownership to an indigenous culture that had no concept that a human could own a tree or a stream.

He dressed in black at all times, dressed well, and always wore a carnation on his lapel. Eventually, those who knew him, especially those acquainted with the shadier side of his business, began to refer to him as the Black Carnation. Anyone who presented as an obstacle or a threat was lost in a mountain canyon or a nearby lake. Others were sold to Shanghai gangs who collected the hapless, to wake up indentured on just such a ship as Bouche had abandoned.

That's where Bouche's partner came into play. On the other side of his coin was the really ugly work. Kikah was a

Native American but not Maidu and not from California. Kikah was from the Shoshone in what is now Northern Nevada. He told Bouche that his Shoshone name was not a good name. Actually, it was a good name that he had disgraced. The sound of it tormented him, and besides, Europeans couldn't pronounce it. Their corruption of that good name only served to exacerbate his agony. He wanted to be called Kick.

Bouche was aware that the European invasion of California had unfavorably impacted the local native Californians. Europeans brought their greed, the concept of ownership, but they also brought measles, diphtheria, smallpox, and syphilis, for which the indigenous people had no defense at all. Encampments were raided. Whole villages disappeared or were displaced. Women were taken and used badly.

Bouche asked Kick why he left his tribe, and he said, "Past is like rocks. Best left where they are." So Bouche did not tell Kick about France or the ship, and Kick never told Bouche about the Shoshone.

That night, long ago on the stormy mountain trail, Kick had decided it was better to try this white man who spoke funny than to continue to wonder where he would be tomorrow. He was tired of running, starving, working... tired of no respect and no future. What could be lost? Time. Time to see if this white man was like the wind or really had a plan. Time to see if he could be trusted. That night in the rain, Kick had looked through the darkness and seen obsession, passion in the blue eyes of Maurice Bouche.

Kick never decided to trust anyone, including Bouche. He learned that as long as he was useful to Bouche, he would not want for much. Kick was particularly useful. While Bouche was flamboyant, Kick was invisible. They were both ruthless, and their partnership flourished in many ways. Kick had no use for most and no mercy for anyone. Bouche provided him with much fuel for the fires of his unhappiness but also an outlet for his rage and need to hurt and destroy. He had a devil in him that was never content.

After the saloon's success, Bouche branched out. He bought land and legitimate businesses, but only those where his growing network of "connections" could be leveraged. Mercantile businesses with a good front made good cover; businesses like salvage, "removal," and small businesses with big back rooms like laundries and liveries. As he built his realm, as Kick handled more and more of the unsavory aspects of the empire, Maurice began to yearn for something else.

California was being tamed. The fast-track conversion of California into the thirty-first state, a free state, in the union of states was not without controversy and exceptions. It was expedited because of the wild and lawless culture surrounding so valuable a region: its coast, timber, water, and gold.

Capitalists were investing in railroads, retail, lumber, and newspapers. Jobs were plentiful. People were prospering. Culture was flourishing. Financiers were opening banks, and the mining industry was expanding the list of treasures in the mountains: silver, copper, and iron, and also gravel, sand, and rock itself. The latter would become the foundation of the new California: cement.

Meanwhile, the population could no longer be contained within the tiny peninsula, so its edges began to fill in with old ships, dirt, pushing out into the massive bay, building higher and more, always more. Too little thought was given to the strata upon which the new empire was being erected. Too *few knew what the Maidu knew: sometimes, the ground is restless. No one asked them.*

Bouche's vision was expanding as well. He wanted to be influential. Not in his world. In the other world, just on the other side, through the invisible wall. The world of commerce, art, music, education, politics, and, yes, law, order. And something else he struggled to put on a list. Maybe he had always wanted these things. Maybe he just never imagined that he could want them.

In 1878, Bouche was in San Francisco and saw something that crystallized his desire. He saw an ankle. It was not the ankle so much as it was what it represented. She was petite, willowy, and refined. She captured his gaze, and he could not get it back. She did not show cleavage. Quite the opposite. She had a small waist, but it was not cinched. She had dark hair, neatly bound at the nape of her neck below a hat that was small and smart. But her face: pale and translucent, like porcelain. And her eyes were bright; from across the street, he could see the brightness of her eyes. When her lips parted slightly into a smile, it was glorious. That ankle, it was the high-button shoe and the pale lace stocking, just a glimpse of the edge of a petticoat. He was transfixed. Long after she had climbed the steps and entered the bank building, Maurice stared after her.

He had a new word to put on his list. It was respectability. He began to take note of his dress and his demeanor. It had to change. For the first time, he noted how the city had changed since he had jumped ship. The population exploded from a couple thousand to twenty-five thousand in just the first couple of years. But that was just the beginning. An entire metropolis had formed in just decades. It had never mattered to him. It was a means to an end. Now, he would make it his new world.

No one from his youth would recognize him now. And, in time, that would change again. Maurice Bouche would change everything! He would become a gentleman, and then he would have a pair of high-button shoes and a laced ankle as well.

7

CAWS FOR HELP

Mason Oeillet bursts open the office door. His sister turns her gaze from the photograph on the wall, and her concentration, to see that trouble has reared its head on her path once again.

"Marie, you have to help me!"

"Really? Do tell," she says with mild indignation, noting that he is disheveled, holding the long nose of a mask in his hand.

"I may have overreacted."

"What a surprise, Mason. What now?" Marie observes that Mason has scratched skin visible above his collar, on his left cheek, and on the back of his hand. Not a good sign. A woman.

"It's that snake, Elyse James. I..." He composes himself. "I may have killed her."

"You what?" She is startled by that word, blinks and pulls in. Yes. He is a spoiled, frightened nine-year-old, as he always morphs when he has really botched something. Quickly, invisibly back in control, she asks, "Well, did you or didn't you? Is she dead?"

"I think so."

"You *think* so?"

"Yes, yes. She's dead. OK, she's dead." Mason does not expect sympathy from Marie, but he is desperate for help. "She threatened me. She threatened all of us. And there she was strutting those tits..." He knew that would not help him. "I'm serious! She has documents. She knows. She is going to tell everything."

"Calm down, you big buffoon. You've killed that reporter. Because she threatened you?"

"She is not just a reporter. She is Logan Malloy's right hand, and now she is the editor and chief of that rag, and she is threatening to do far worse than Malloy ever did! She thinks she's a player, and she is going to upset the plans."

"I think you mean to use the past tense. Apparently, she has no thoughts at all now. Plans? What plans?"

"I am trying to stop your ridiculous husband from interfering with the casino. I want that casino. I have a huge stake in that casino. I had a plan. It would have worked, to stop your husband from squelching that casino! You have no idea what I've done to prevent that."

Marie has turned with her feet into her high heels, standing now, facing her brother straight on. She is taller than he. He barely notices. "Let me see if I can lace up that rambling regurgitated pap into something intelligible. You had some scheme with that odious newspaper owner that you thought would discourage Atticus from doing everything he can to stop that casino. Am I right so far?"

Mason nods, feeling the cold cut of Marie's wit dissecting the situation.

"And that reporter, editor, whatever, threatened those plans? So you've killed her?"

"No." He sighs. The last person on earth he wants to explain this to is Marie. But he is in trouble, and there is no one better able to help him than Marie. If she will. He feels overwhelmed, fraught, and just smart enough to realize that he has really screwed up this time with no idea how to make this one go away. He inhales deeply and begins again. "Look, I've been doing Elyse for a while now." Marie just glares without surprise. "I may have worked on Malloy to move her up, but that's not the point. I was working with Malloy to threaten your husband with exposure of his—"

"Yes. I can imagine. You can skip that part."

"It was working."

"No, it wasn't. But go on."

"What do you mean? It would have worked. That pansy asshole would not like being exposed for the queer that he is, jumping from bed to bed all over the place."

Marie's face tightens just a bit, and she squints. "You really are an idiot, Mason."

"He didn't like it. He told Logan that she better not go through with the story. He was pissed! He would have backed off. Then the casino would go in…"

"We can discuss how you completely, unfailingly misinterpret things later. But go on with the killing part."

"I arranged to meet her up on the private floor, for some fun." Marie sighs, bored and wishing Mason had a modicum of succinct articulation at his disposal. "But right off the top, she starts with this 'Logan's dead and I'm in charge' bullshit. She tells me that she is altering the plan. *She!* That was bad enough, but then she hands me this paper." He tries to hand it to Marie.

Marie doesn't reach for it at all. She says instead, "I'm not touching anything a dead girl gave you, moron. What is it? What does it say?"

"It is a summary of the Black Carnation, and, well, it is an expose on where the family jewels originated, you know, the whole dirty mess. And she wasn't aiming at me. She was aiming at Maurice Oeillet, Uncle Maurie. She isn't after me. She's after the Oeillet family."

"For what?"

"Fifty million."

"And your counteroffer, your solution, was to kill her?"

"There was more. I can't explain. I was drunk. She was... You had to be there."

"So grateful I was not. So where did this outrageous overreaction take place?"

"Upstairs."

"You really are the stupidest Oeillet that ever lived." She pauses and looks into her brother's face and contemplates how this *could* ruin everything. She would have to try to help this absolute idiot before he brought them all down. The last fragmented scrap of a childhood memory arises: Mason as a hapless, spoiled, incompetent boy—for whom she might have had a fragmented scrap of sympathy. But in the blink of an eye, that vanishes. "Where is this... dead person... now?"

"In Room 533. Come up with me and tell me what to do. I'll do whatever you say!"

Marie smiles and almost imperceptibly shakes her head. "Do you actually think, even for a moment, that I would accompany you to the scene of a crime? I won't go anywhere near that room. Not one skin cell of mine will ever land on the carpet of the hallway, let alone that room."

"Do you want me to take photos?"

"Are you still drunk, or are you actually this brainless? Never mind. It is almost impossible for you to escape what you have done. You were far too foolish, and you are far too incompetent to erase all the errors you have made—partially because you are incapable of even knowing what they are. I will tell you what you must do, but first, which elevator did you use?"

"Private."

"One tiny point for you. And how is it you got from the private elevator to the ballroom?"

"Outside staircase to the pool."

"That's on camera." She pauses, doing the math. "Here's the equation, and everything from here on has to solve in this fashion. You stayed the night here at the resort. You got up and came down here. That is all chiseled in stone. This will be messy. Perhaps not fifty million messy, but it will be expensive. Your *friend* will be on camera until she entered the private elevator. So we have to misdirect where she went on the private floor. Let me guess, wild-ass speculation, you screwed her as well?" Mason doesn't answer other than with his face and body language. "Of course. Well, this will be the worst ever. And when it's over, you will pay, brother dear. And I will take the pound of flesh of my choosing."

That makes Mason shiver inside as he replies, "Anything."

"Think. Exactly what did you do from the moment you put the key in the lock until you stepped on that staircase. Everything! We have until the crew comes up to the fifth floor at noon to work miracles."

"Oh. I put the Do Not Disturb on the door."

"Yes. Well, you are down here, recorded by camera at almost 3:00 a.m., and you don't get that the sign on the door is part of your stupidity?"

Nothing but Flounce

Henry Oeillet rose from the chair of honor with the help of his great-grandson, Maurice Oeillet, and shuffled toward the President of the University of Northern California, East Bay, to the thunderous applause of an audience there to celebrate the opening of the new medical school, funded by the Oeillet Foundation.

Legitimacy had cost dearly in the beginning. But it served as all things do. He appeared in good society as a man with modest means who was eager and willing to establish himself. He had reserves when it was critical. In those days, no one asked too many questions about where the capital came from—so long as it was available and momentous when applied. And after the earthquake, it was desperately needed. Thus, Henry made his debut in San Francisco society.

Henry's wits were slicing in new directions: finance, industry, and charity. Always charity. He learned about the power of doing good, the influence it wielded, the ability it had to silence objection and obliterate those with more selfish motives. He learned, too, the power that the appearance of goodwill held in the hearts and minds of the public. You didn't have to accomplish good. Just speak of good, be on the right side of any issue with compassion, appear to do good in selfless altruism that provokes awe and respect and way too few questions, and paint an impervious veneer of righteousness and legitimacy.

It didn't matter that rescue missions did as much harm as good and often became harbors for the ne'er-do-well and hangers-on. It didn't matter that drunks rarely achieved sobriety, and behind the scenes, you dealt in bootleg liquor. It didn't matter that the lazy were not stupid but rather accomplished at taking any and every free pass. In fact, shelters actually encourage the incorrigible and provide no incentive to strive or motivation to achieve. All the more compelling the need for charity. It was a beautiful cycle of dependency and mechanism to ensure dependence. And it also created an army of the smart and manipulative.

None of that mattered because Henry believed the public did not want to be involved with the unfortunate. He attributed the average person with feelings of guilt. Some feel it more than others. Most not enough to give what they have to others. Nonetheless, many want to feel better about the situation, assuage their guilt; they are compelled to do something. Some give of themselves, their time, and their hearts. Others just want to believe that good is being done in their name and that the unfortunate are "taken care of." They prefer to give a portion of what they have in the form of money. But they really want others to give and give big. They cheer them on and endorse their giving, never asking too many questions or demanding accountability.

In this way, legitimacy was bought and paid for, and over a second lifetime, Henry became a highly-respected businessman, financier, known for his modesty, always shunning any spotlight. Selfless humility and generosity were the hallmarks of his image. It quickly became apparent that he valued the ear of politicians, and his generosity extended to them as well. Over his second life, Henry became the silent puppeteer behind Sacramento. This became his most profitable endeavor yet, on many levels.

Henry was old and had little time left, but he was gratified to see his family so honored and the name Oeillet engraved on the stone façade of the new building. It didn't bother him that most Americans pronounced his invented name incorrectly. It added to the distance between him and his past. When he was greeted, "Mr. Willet!" he simply smiled and nodded. He knew the meaning of his name. He knew all too well who he was. In fact, who he had been never left him. It lived in his black heart and in his dreams.

When the beautiful plaque was handed to him, he gestured for his great-grandson to receive it. The president had spoken of the great changes that had taken place in the state of California, the future of change ahead. Henry Oeillet smiled at the idea of change and the depth of its meaning. That evening, there was a banquet, and Henry's entire family was there, including his wife. Her dark hair was now white, and her face was aged. She no longer wore high-button shoes, but she still had the look of a porcelain doll.

Henry had lived an adventurous, dangerous, and powerful life. He thought of the général whose wrath had launched his life and did not give a thought to oppressors and abusers. He no longer remembered what it was like to be anything but the personification of iron will to rise above. The table had tall vases filled with carnations with orange blossoms draping down to the table. White carnations. For a brief moment, he saw fire and intelligence shining back from black eyes. He stiffened all his features, and his body became rigid. His eyes darted for a second.

Marie, his wife, touched his arm, "Are you alright, Henry?"

He looked into her face and regained himself. "Yes. Fine. Just a momentary twinge. Nothing." Henry wondered if Kick would chase him into hell to get his revenge. Or was it just his own culpable soul, the conscience he never had, catching up to him in his final days?

More and more, in the night, faces visited him. It was increasingly difficult to hold himself together. He felt he had to use all his strength to keep the faces at bay. Moments like this, where his acquired legitimacy was affirmed, helped. But only for a brief time. Then the faces returned. Occasionally, they spoke to him, pleas, last words, accusations. It was maddening, and all he could do to resist them—taking him over, possessing him, destroying him.

Several months passed from the dedication, and the faces grew more persistent, the voices deafening. He lived in the confines of his mind, unable to reach out into his life, to participate, to enjoy anything. He wanted to cry out, cover his ears, blind his eyes, to have his wife tell him that everything was all right. He wanted someone, something to stop the faces, the voices. But he was helpless. Trapped alone with himself. His silence was baffling to his physician. He drifted in and out of consciousness and always awoke short of breath, stressed. His doctor and the family presumed he was suffering from stroke, hemorrhage, or some form of apoplexy. Until one night.

Henry awoke, sat up screaming in his bed, fighting for his life. Marie came rushing in. He looked at her, arms bracing for attack, appeared to shape a word with his mouth, and collapsed. Marie was momentarily excited that he was animated. It was short-lived. He was dead. Marie looked into his face, alarmed. His visage was contorted even in death. His eyes were open, wide and fixed in a terrified stare. In time, as the blood stilled, as the oxygen content of the cells was depleted, the musculature let go, and his body, his face, and his hands eased.

8

PLAYING WITH MATCHES

Sheriff Noble and Lieutenant Riley are at the Butte County Morgue before the sun rises. Information is available, and they are both eager to learn how to proceed.

"Sir, I want to get back up there as soon as possible. Rodriguez is up there on his own with a lot to hold on to by himself," Lieutenant Riley stated as she and the sheriff pushed through the double stainless-steel doors. But I am also eager for something to go on. Yesterday was frustrating."

The sheriff hears the formal "sir," and it pains, but he swallows it. "For me, too. To say the least. Actually, it was a bit embarrassing even. I thought we were on to something with Flynn. Anyway, in my gut, I really like him for this, but for the moment, we got nothing. I don't want to go through that again. My fault, Riley." Sheriff Noble is not happy about backtracking in front of Lieutenant Riley, but he is too forthright to cower from what happened. "Too eager to act on impulse, what I assumed in my mind was genuine. A lesson. For both of us."

Lauren Riley watches him confess and feels admiration that he effortlessly takes possession of what was a misstep. She sees her sheriff as brave and genuine. She likes him. A lot.

She also knows that any feelings beyond that are disastrous—in every single regard. Especially for her. If she allowed it, she would tell him what she is thinking; she would let him see how pleased she is to be working at his side. She is aware of the tension between them. But Lieutenant Riley is resolute and counters such feelings with decorum. It is a shield.

"This morning, they all will be recovering from last night's gala," Jason continues. "The road hasn't opened, and it won't until we open it. Nothing's flying, boating, or rolling. So it's a captive enclave for now."

The Butte County Morgue/Forensic Lab is essential in the North Valley because prior to the new lab, there was no investigative lab anywhere, and local law enforcement throughout the valley had to conduct autopsies at the local mortuaries and send out evidence to commercial labs on contract for analysis. They had no control and had to rely on strict requirements, audits, and face tough questions if cases went to court.

Once the morgue and lab were built, Butte County could act as a central resource for their adjacent jurisdictions. Doctor Chen is the chief medical examiner and supervises the lab. He enters with the preliminary report and hands each of them a copy. "Let's go in here so we can discuss what we have so far." Chen gestures to the interview room. "Not a lot, but what we have is interesting. Straight into the heart and out the back at a slightly elevated angle, not much."

"How tall was the victim?"

"Five-ten, wearing heels—and she was."

"Now that is interesting. Flynn is five-six, according to his driver's license."

"The bullet recovered outside the shattered window is a 45. Probably a Colt revolver. Six narrow grooves 1:16 and a left-hand twist."

"Stretched?" Riley says.

"Some," Dr. Chen replies.

"Stretched?" Sheriff queries.

Riley looks at the sheriff's smile and reruns the past twenty-four hours in her mind. She smiles. "Well, it's something I heard yesterday that kind of stuck in my mind."

"Continue, Doctor, please. This is good," the sheriff said.

"Old?" Riley inquires.

"Yes. Probably quite old."

"Yes?" Sheriff echoes as a question.

"By the way," Riley queries, "why'd the window fall?"

"Good question. But the answer is simple. Ever read the warranty of safety glass? Guaranteed not to fall... and then the disclaimers start. One of them is a penetration, and another is temperature and pressure. The bullet was compounded by cold and wind. And then there are the flaws in installation and maintenance clause, etc. They fall occasionally. They are not perfect.

"Speaking of glass, there's more." Chen continues. "Two glasses. One was shattered on the floor with the window. It fell from a height enough to smash it. I'd say it was in our victim's hand. At the scene, it probably didn't stand out, but once we had unbagged all the glass, well, it was obvious that there were two. I swabbed the larger pieces of the shattered glass. It had held gin and a hint of vermouth. Confirmed by the fact that the victim ate cheese, crackers as her last meal. And the odor of the stomach content indicates alcohol."

"Nutritious. The other glass?"

"Only fingerprint we could get was Malloy's. No help there. It held wine. The wine in the bottle on the table. But I swabbed what I could of the other glass that broke on the table for DNA. It is clean. I'd say she was expecting someone to join her, and maybe they did. One way or the other, that person did not drink—at least not out of that glass."

"Did the person arrive and shoot her instead of joining her?"

"Or did they never arrive? Or did they arrive after Malloy was shot? And if so, why didn't they call it in? What were they expecting to do? Did they do it?" Riley queries.

"Yes. All good questions," the sheriff says.

"And those are for you guys to answer, but I may be able to help," Doctor Chen chimes in. "First, we got some prints around, not Malloy's. Several. Working on that. All that will prove is that someone was there in her house at some time or other. But we'll see what we get."

"That could be important. What else?" the sheriff acknowledges.

"We got tire tread images. Four, actually."

"How'd you do that?" the lieutenant inquires, impressed.

"Well, I didn't do it, but ice is a funny business. It freezes and gets crunched and freezes again, but unless it melts and returns to liquid, there is always some solid that remains. Where it doesn't get crunched, if it is cold enough, the structure remains. Have to do it with digital photography because of the temperatures. But a digital photograph, if done well, is better than a casting.

"Now that doesn't mean we got great tread," Chen continues. "But we got some undamaged digital structures, some overrun, layers, all the way to the ground. Another advantage is the cold. Can't cast, but if the snow is light, in some cases, it can be dusted. Most not useful at all, and some, well, four distinct, I think we can work with."

"So what you're saying is that after the snow began that night, at least four vehicles drove up and down that drive?

That's sixteen tires times two, up and back total. OK. I'm impressed," the sheriff clarified.

"Yes. Miraculous even. Be sure to pass that on to the team that got the shots. That took patience and a bit of luck. I mean, think of it. Each ice crystal is a mirror. The lighting—"

"I get it. Miraculous. I will commend them. But what do we have?" the sheriff interrupted.

"OK. In the process of traveling, three left us at least a trace of tread that was not totally obliterated by the others, the subsequent snow, etc. Yes."

"Was one of them Malloy's vehicle?" the lieutenant queried.

"No. We checked. That I can tell you."

"Four. Of course, one was the housekeeper's on the top," the lieutenant added.

"The Ford Escort with chains."

"Yes. That's right," the lieutenant affirms.

"What helped is one tread is the chains; that really left three tread patterns. One is fairly weak, so don't count on that. That leaves two very useful structures. Here's the list of possible matches."

"List? Wow, and it's not a short list either."

"I said we got images. Not the best. But, of course, bring me the tires, and we can make a match. One thing I can tell you is two are high-end snow tires. To put either of those tires on a vehicle would cost more than my old clunker is worth. So that should narrow it down. The vehicles that put them on at the factory are listed."

"Two lists?"

"The short one is for the high-end tread, and the longer one is for the others—but since you know who drove the chains, well, like I said, narrows it down."

"The fragments in the victim's hand are interestingly the withered petals of a flower. A carnation, actually. The same petals that were scattered, frozen on the floor. So why ever she did it, she grabbed a carnation as she was shot because she went fast and had only a second or two to do anything."

"Maybe she was holding it when she was shot?"

"Unlikely. If she was, she had the flower itself in the grip of her fist and crushed it."

"Huh."

"I know the wheels in your head are turning, Riley. Whatcha got?"

"I haven't got anything. Just some things are nudging me a little. Can't put it together yet. One of the team at Moluku Lake PD was pulling the registrations for everyone on our immediate list, so we start with that list," Riley suggested.

"Agreed. Thanks, Doctor! Let me know when you get more."

"Of course," Chen said as the two got up to depart.

Riley sends a text as she walks out with Sheriff Noble. "OK. Just a question in my mind."

"Go," the sheriff affirms.

"When we met with Marie Flynn yesterday, she said that her husband had a gun collection. Maybe there are some antiques? Maybe an old Colt single-action revolver? I think we should check that out."

"Indeed. And high-end vehicles, that starts to point to a distinctive crowd, of which Atticus Flynn is its poster boy. Maybe we should dig into that iron-clad alibi. Money buys alibis. Tell you what, I'll take Flynn's gun collection. You take the alibi."

"I didn't expect you to return, sir."

Jason wasn't going to let go of this for layers of reasons. "Normally, I wouldn't. But this one is compelling. I want one more opportunity at Flynn."

"Got a little under your skin, uh?" she gently needles.

Sheriff Noble laughs big and unrestrained. "Yes. That was annoying." Lauren likes his laugh. "I got caught off guard, and I got had. And if he had anything to do with this, I will take great satisfaction hearing those cuffs lock. I admit it. But next time, I will *know* it is him and we got the nut!"

"Reassuring to know it happens even to someone like you." Lauren is gratified but also pleased to know he has no need to duck or make a pretense of excuse. He just owns it. She isn't sure she could be so confident. She also knows that it is with experience that wisdom comes to us all. She longs for wisdom. The contemplation of wisdom brings one person front and center in her mind.

"It's not in the opening play, Riley. It's in the last hand of the game."

Riley's phone notifies her a text has arrived. "It's the registrations." She scans the list of vehicles and finds seven *very* high-end options: some Cads, Mercedes. "OK, this will qualify as high-end: an H2 Land Rover, a Lamborghini, a couple Ferraris—oh!—and a Rolls-Royce Cullinan. Wow! These are... wow. That Cullinan is a couple years of my salary."

"And the who's?"

"Maybe we can rule out the roadsters unless we find one of them that looks like it took on a blizzard. That leaves Land Rover, ah, Atticus Flynn—his is a Range Rover P525 HSE. H2, that's Mason Oeillet. The Cullinan, none other than Jayden Listeri! And the list. Apparently, both the Range Rover and the Cullinan could have been at Logan Malloy's that night."

"Then we absolutely need to tear apart that alibi!"

Riley says, "I think Kevin, my partner, should do that! He's a bit of a bulldog."

They head back up the mountain, passing the Butte County Public Works vehicles clearing the road, further on to where the road was not groomed in Plumas County, heading toward impassable, which is fine with Sheriff Noble. His service vehicle can make it. Highway patrol will make sure no one else does.

All In

Maurice Bouche invited Kick to accompany him up the canyon. They went on horseback. "Been a decade since I've been up there. I want to see it one more time, but I don't look forward to the solitude. Come with me, for old times' sake." Bouche had an assignment south in the big valley for Kick that next week. Kick was going on the train on Monday, would be gone for a while.

Kick was glad to go south, interested in the train ride. He agreed to the canyon trip since they would return in time for him to catch the Southern Pacific run south. Kick was thinking about the future. Bouche was withdrawn, sullen lately. Kick wondered what plot Bouche could be hatching.

He was working on one of his own. Kick had heard of a gang of robbers in the Bay Area plaguing the Southern Pacific. Disgruntled former employees: angry, vengeful. Kick was thinking of this when Bouche told him he would send him south via train. Kick was nervous. Something was different, and since Kick had never fully trusted Bouche, he wasn't going to wait around to see how that played out for him. He already knew that he was not included in the early planning, but that was not new. Kick agreed to the canyon as a last chance to figure out what was happening before he deserted Bouche and took a different path. Kick was cautious and leery.

They set out into the mountains, along the old Feather River trail traveled so long ago. Kick observed that, in many ways, not a thing had changed. But then they came to beds of rock into which tracks had been laid, obstructions, bridges, or diversions. There was the handprint of the Europeans.

Kick had come to the same work camp that Bouche had decades ago. Kick had signed on because he was hungry and tired of running. He did not leave the Shoshone. They exiled him. Subsequently, Kikah learned that some of the young men from his tribe, less forgiving than the Council, had determined to end his exile forever. Kikah moved west and south to escape their hunt.

He didn't like rules, and he didn't respect his family or the tribe. This made him an outsider early in life. He resented any discipline and resisted the rituals that made up the Shoshone culture. One of the tribal fathers whom Kikah had most egregiously offended had told him that he had an evil spirit in him. That leader told the tribal council that his name should be changed from Kikah, which means snake, to Jahabich, which means devil. The tribal council was saddened that such a request would be made and determined to let this shameful thing be a turning point for the young man.

So the Council let Kikah leave, in exile, with his good name intact in the hope that, as a result, he would turn his life around, find his spirit guide, and return to his tribe and family someday. It became so.

But Kikah turned even darker and embraced the devil the elder had seen in him. Snakes are admired for their stealth, their power, and their beauty. He had liked his name. Now it became a reminder that he was unworthy of his beautiful name. It would pain him whenever it was used.

At nightfall, Bouche selected a grove of trees similar to the one in which the two men had met long ago. It was not storming, it was fall, and Bouche indicated that Kick should seek firewood while he took care of the horses for the night.

By firelight, Bouche gave a bottle of whiskey, with one for himself. He gave Kick his train ticket, a bag of gold, and $10,000. He told Kick that he wanted him to have a good life and that he was considering an alteration in his own life. One that would lead away from the empire of the Black Carnation they had built together.

Bouche told Kick about his new life. He said it would be in San Francisco. Bouche told Kick his new name and how he had been slowly establishing his new identity: an address, bills, a club, all in the name of Henry Oeillet. They had a laugh about the fact that his new name was French for "spring, renewal, specifically the carnation." They laughed and drank to new lives!

He told Kick about the beautiful girl he had fallen in love with, the daughter of a banker named DePaschi. He told Kick that the father was a bit of a scallywag himself. He regaled with a brief history of banking at the beginning of the gold rush. The only prerequisite was that you had a large safe and kept the combination to yourself. They both laughed and had a good swig.

Over time, DePaschi had grown rich and had many banks in the city. Now he was a respected, powerful, and legitimate member of the banking community. Bouche said that although he was an important man, he understood the struggle and guts to make tough choices. They drank to men of the world, to the strength to choose, to men with money, pretty daughters... and then they drank again to having lots of money!

Bouche said he wanted to take care of Kick. Kick looked into the eyes of Bouche and considered if he had been wrong to withhold his trust all these years. "Is this an end for us?" Kick inquired.

"Think of it as the beginning of a new and easier existence, my friend."

"We have never been friends."

"Perhaps we will become friends." They drank to better days ahead.

Kick had never had a friend. This was not what he had anticipated. He felt he had to be honest if he was going to have a friend. He told Bouche that he had also dreamed of a new life. He didn't share that his dream had been of a new venture in crime. He didn't share his mistrust, his ill feelings of late. He just said that he had dreams, and he thanked his partner for the help in getting started. He never thought of a life without rage, without bloodshed. It wasn't in his nature to imagine life within the fabric of society. Any society. It was frightening. It was also intriguing. Almost appealing.

The two men drank into the evening, under the stars, shared secrets, and fell asleep at this monumental shift in the relationship. Kick felt that it was possible to have something he had never experienced: hope.

Kick awoke to a tiny sound. His eyes opened and barely focused on Bouche's upside-down face above him. Bouche held the bowie knife above his own head as it came down into Kick's chest, piercing the skin, forcing through the interstitial tissue, scraping his ribs, and directly into his heart with gravity and the full collapse of Bouche's weight behind it. He responded with the instinct to roll, spring into action, and fight, but none of these commands ever reached his body.

Bouche knew that Kick could not be a part of his new life. He also realized that regardless of how Kick might feel about it that today, in time, without some manner of influence governing his choices, Kick would end up causing Henry Oeillet a problem. And Kick would be a messy, big problem.

Kick had been an invaluable asset. It was a loss. But Kick had no possible redemption in the world to which Henry Oeillet aspired. It was better this way. The journey south would cover the fact that Kick was gone for anyone who noticed. The fact that he didn't return would go unnoticed as Maurice Bouche vanished from the hills and was reinvented in the city. Bouche took back the money, the gold, and burned the ticket, and slowly, relentlessly, the body of the devil.

9

SETTING BACK BURNS

"When did you arrive at the airport?"

"I was there at 7:45. It's all recorded in GPS. You can verify," the chauffer replied.

"And I will. When was Flynn's flight due in?" Rodriguez returned.

"7:52, and it's never early. Often late."

"And it was late that night?"

"Yes. An hour. I was tracking the flight to be sure I was there on time. The report of delay didn't come until I was already on my way to the airport. As it turned out, I had time to grab food and coffee and still had to wait. They must have hit the storm late in the flight."

"When did you pick him up?"

"He had carry-on, so he came straight to the car at the curb within fifteen minutes of the plane landing. Shortly after nine."

"And you drove directly to Moluku?"

"We drove through a Starbucks to get more coffee and food for the drive. Then directly home. There were cameras."

"Traffic?"

"Bay Area. Not good, even at that hour. It is usually four hours. It was longer. Cameras at all the toll booths—time stamps."

"Did you make any other stops?"

"Gas. At the Casino in Oroville, starting up the hill."

"Atticus Flynn stopped for gas at the Casino in Oroville?"

He chuckled. "Yeah. It is the cheapest gas," he shrugged.

Deputy Rodriguez just smiled. "Getting you to the Flynn estate at..."

"About 2:30ish. I didn't know at the time I'd need to be precise, but it is all in the GPS record, as I've said."

"And are you an employee of the Flynn estate?"

"No. I am an employee of the lodge."

"Get bonuses much?"

"Yes, and generous tips, and, yes, I do favors for our guests—especially the boss of all bosses. But no. I didn't take a dime to make any of this up."

"It is possible that you made the trip to and from without a passenger."

"Yes. But how would Atticus Flynn get from the airport to Moluku Lake in a blizzard without me? Airport is closed. Had to be vehicle. So what is your point?"

"Any other vehicles or drivers make that trek?"

"I can't say. Easy for you to check."

"Would you lie for him?"

"Probably, maybe. Depends." He pauses and looks directly at the deputy. "But I am not lying."

Rodriguez sits calmly and assesses the young man. He looks at his dress, his posture, his arms, hands, demeanor, and into his eyes.

"Tell me again about your evening the night Malloy was murdered."

"Worked until ten. I was seen by many of my staff during the evening," Jayden replies smugly and glances at his surroundings without moving his head or shoulders. "Commercial, dull, green everything," he thinks. Jayden Listeri was invited, sort of. He does not like it. He was driven by a polite but firm Moluku Lake police officer to the station, preferring that no one witness the "escort." This was one headline for which he was not eager.

"Did any of them or anyone else see you leave?" Riley inquires.

"The security camera in the executive garage, Officer."

"Lieutenant, actually. We'll get the garage footage. Then what?"

"I went home to my loft."

"No. That is a lie. Want to try again?"

"I didn't park in the garage. So I won't be on the camera there."

"You went to Logan Malloy's house."

"I did not."

"You did, and I can prove it, Listeri, so let's just go there, and you tell me what happened. Did Flynn send you?"

"Logan Malloy does not have a security system." He chuckles. "And we can see—now vividly—what that leads to. So you cannot prove I was there."

"Leads to what?"

"Murder. Do keep up."

Riley smiles. "Your car was. And it left tire tracks."

"It was snowing. You can't have tire tracks. And if you do, useless in court. My attorneys will eat it for a snack."

"We have tread in digital image that match your Rolls. We are impounding your Cullinan right now to verify. And, yes.

Here's your copy of the warrant to do so, along with the reasoning. Maybe your attorney better catch his snack on the way to court. What do ya think, Jayden?"

Jayden Listeri's face loses its smugness for a moment. It is replaced with a placid smile that draws slowly across the lower portion of his face. "The Cullinan?"

"Yes. And we'll dump the GPS while we're at it, so you might as well tell us what happened. You went there to confront her over the article she was about to publish, right?"

"Actually," he pauses, "I did. OK. Yes. That's it. But she was dead when I got there! Swear!"

"Why didn't you just say that in the first place? See, 'cause now I don't believe you."

"Why in the world would I risk everything to kill her when she was my cheapest form of advertisement?"

"Because all the advertising in the world cannot make up for the scandal over Atticus Flynn about to break."

"Atticus?" His shoulders relax a bit, and he leans back. His mind is shifting tracks. "Yes. Atticus. Well, who really cares about that, really, these days? Gossip, she had no proof. It was just going to be a flashy tabloid piece, what she was best at. Maybe I just wanted to see it before she blew it out there. I wouldn't kill her or anyone. Certainly not over an affair with a married man."

"Well, Atticus Flynn is not just a married man. The Flynns are not *just* a married couple. And what about Marie Flynn?" She paused, recording his reactions, then continued. "Would you do it for Atticus? I am quite sure that Atticus would not want people to know that Marie Flynn is merely his beard."

Listeri smiles at the idea of Marie Flynn: beard. "Kill for Atticus? You must mistake sex for devotion or something. Me? In prison, the result of a gay scandal? Oh, that would make for a fabulous lifestyle—and for God knows how long! Never! You are way off base, out of the ballpark, in some other universe than mine, honey!"

Riley considers the depth of arrogance and self-centered indulgence that is seated across from her at that moment. She decides that Jayden Listeri is not a likely candidate for a hitman for Atticus Flynn or anyone else. "Tell me exactly what happened." It occurs to her that if Mrs. Flynn could hear this interview, she might buy a hit on Listeri. Then an image of Marie Flynn flashes in her mind, and she figures that she would not.

"I drove up, presuming she was in her house, drinking martinis, working. I went to the door to ring the bell, but the door was ajar. I pushed it open with my elbow."

"And why would you do that if you presumed she was just inside doing her thing?"

"The door ajar was odd. Odd implies something out of the ordinary. I was cautious from that moment on."

"But you went in."

"Yes."

"And?"

"The wind was blowing, snow blowing in, she's dead on the floor, outrageously displayed, face up, eyes open, blood, gauche pink negligee—"

"Were the eyes glazed?"

"I don't recall that they were. Not that I look at corpses and notice right away if their eyes are glazed... as a rule," he says sarcastically.

"Why didn't you call someone?"

"She was dead. Who should I call? You? So I could endure this? Please. I went into her office to see if there was a printout of the article. There wasn't that I could see, but what a mess! I would have grabbed the thumb drive, but there wasn't one. I probably would have turned on her laptop to look at what she was working on, but it was on the floor." He chuckles and gives a flippant, dismissive gesture with his hand. "So, I left."

"What time was that, precisely?"

"Well, precisely, I opened the door at about 10:40. It took a while even in my vehicle to get up there in the storm, with the roads and the snow. 10:50 latest. I didn't think to look at the time. I did when I got home, and it was midnight. I parked on the street just so I wouldn't trigger the garage cameras or the time stamp. There you have it."

With the roads blocked, every room in town is full, and the traffic in and out of cafés, restaurants, and the lodge is heavy. Throngs at a time, in their parkas, full-length down coats, faux fur and real fur, gloves, hoods, hats, and snow boots. In fact, the only differentiation from one creature to the next is the variations in the garments that obscure them otherwise. Once inside, they defrock and can be distinguished.

In Oeufs et Crème that morning, the crowd is slow to build. Many of the guests are having breakfast in their rooms, and those who rise, dress, and come downstairs do so at a leisurely pace.

There is nowhere for them to head out. Drivers have been given the morning off, and their passengers have no exodus plans. But once the crowd builds, it is demanding. The waitlist is an hour out, so many are in the main gathering room with the sky-high copper chimney, radiating heat and ambiance while they inquire, complain, gossip, and sip Kioki coffee, espressos, and cappuccinos. Trays of delectable pastries are circulating to offset any inconvenience, all compliments of Oeufs et Crème. It is festive at the moment.

Betsy, on the other hand, left the lodge the previous evening, paid her babysitter, put her daughter to sleep, and spent an hour with Howard before crashing. Now she is back working a hectic shift, tired, hoping for her dream job at Agile Noir. "Morning, sir. Coffee? Espresso?"

"Neither. But a moment of your time." His eyes are riveting.

Betsy says, "Beg your pardon?"

He still has his coat on and the hood pulled all the way out, so it shades, obscuring the features of his face. He smiles reassuringly. "My dear, I want you to listen to me, but I also want you to smile and act as if I am giving you my breakfast order. Is that clear?"

Betsy frowns and leans in. "I don't understand, sir."

"You will. If you value your daughter, you will do as I say."

Betsy's frown flickers, deepens then deliberately turns into a smile. Her eyes glance left and right, and she doesn't know what to do. So she fixes her smile and listens attentively.

Sheriff Jason Noble knocks on the impressive glass door of the Flynn mansion. A small lady wearing a crisp uniform answers the door.

"Good morning, I am Sheriff Noble, and I want to speak with Atticus Flynn."

"I am sorry. Mr. Flynn is not up at this time."

"When will he be up?"

"I am not sure."

"I think you can get him up for this."

"I cannot, sir. Mr. Dawson is out right now, and I cannot do that."

"Dawson?"

"Mr. Dawson, the butler. He is out at the moment."

"What's your name?"

"Lydia, sir."

"Lydia, either you go up and wake Mr. Flynn, or you get Mr. Dawson or anyone else to do it, or I will go up myself with my handcuffs out. Do you understand?"

"Yes, sir." She does not invite him inside the door. He is patient.

Another lady in a nice dress comes to the door with Lydia behind her. "How can I help you, Officer?"

"Sheriff. Sheriff Noble, and I need to speak to Atticus Flynn. Now."

"Please come in." She crisply directs the sheriff to a sitting room off the entrance, and both of them seem to disappear. It is ten minutes before Atticus Flynn descends the staircase. He is in silk pajamas and a matching robe, slippers, but does not look as if he has just stirred from sleep. He comes directly into the sitting room, does not even glance at the sheriff, and takes a seat without offering one to Jason. Promptly, a small cup of espresso, on a saucer, with a small spoon, and two sugar cubes, is placed in his hands. He does not say a word, stirs in the sugar, inhales the rich aroma that even Jason can smell, lets the breath out, takes a sip, and returns the cup to the saucer, which he holds with both hands between him and the sheriff. "Well?"

The sheriff watches all of this, measuring the disdain that radiates from this little man. Jason doesn't mind that he is irritated. He decides to work it a bit more. "Gosh, that smells great," the sheriff says, smiling, nodding. "I think I'd enjoy a cup. Make mine American and black."

Atticus looks back, for the first time, making eye contact. Perturbed but unruffled. "Of course, Sheriff. Anything else?" Atticus nods to Lydia, who, it turns out, is quietly just outside the room. She leaves her post, presumably to fetch Jason's coffee.

"Now that you have inserted yourself into my otherwise relaxed morning, how can I help you?"

"I wanted to let you know that we have verified your alibi for the Malloy murder. Sure would appear that you were indeed on your way back from the airport that night. We even caught a glimpse of you in the backseat at one of the toll booths." He winks.

"Oh, I'm so relieved," Atticus replies facetiously.

"Still working on the angle that you paid someone to do it. I just love you for this. I think you know that. But if you didn't do it, if you didn't pay someone, who do you think did it?"

"I'm sure I don't have a clue. She had more enemies than most. The list is long. I don't envy you that."

"Thank you for your concern. She was killed with a 45 pistol. Colt 45 single-action revolver. Know anyone who owns one of those?"

With that, Atticus's brow furrows a bit, and his eyes look to the left. Then with a small flick of his brow, he brings them back to the sheriff. "You know that I own one, I'm sure."

"Yes. Got your records right here on my phone. No permits."

"Antiques don't require permits."

"Gun sales are recorded. Especially notable ones. And you have quite a collection, it appears. Let's have a look at it."

"You got a warrant?"

"Yes. I do."

"Well then. Shall we?" Flynn rises from the chair and heads down the hall to the "gun room."

As Jason follows, Lydia arrives and offers, "American, black." Jason lifts the cup off the saucer in his stride and continues directly behind Flynn.

On one wall is an enormous gun safe. Adorning the walls in locked glass cases is the most impressive antique gun collection Jason has ever personally seen. Atticus does not have a Colt 45 single-action revolver, he has half a dozen, and he has all the predecessors as well, neatly displayed with plaques in order. There they are. Six beautiful old weapons. They are each unique: beautiful, engraved whalebone, ivory, or wood grips. Some of the barrels are also engraved. Gorgeous. Jason wants to abandon his mission and admire, handle each one.

But one catches Jason's eye. It is plain, perhaps the oldest. Plain walnut grip, smooth from use. It has been fired many times, cleaned, polished, and fired again. The pistol has a patina that ranges from blue to pewter, with much of it a rich, warm brown. Jason wants to touch it. Just to touch it. He shrugs off a deeper, more covetous thought and says, "We will be taking every one of the Colts in to be tested. My team will be here shortly. You'll get a receipt. We'll take good care of them, I assure you."

"Does someone like you have any idea how much they are worth?"

"Probably more than I can imagine."

"It is not just money. They are history. They are magnificent devices, each with a story, each one deadly. Each one worthy of deference."

"Doesn't matter. If one of them shot Logan Malloy, we'll soon know it. You want to tell me about that now before we find the murder weapon?"

"Sheriff, there is nothing to tell. What in the name of the Almighty would cause you to think, for one minute, that I would use my own gun to commit murder—or allow one of them to be used in such a distasteful encounter?"

"People with lethal hatred. People committing murder rarely think it through carefully, rarely do the rational thing. That works to our advantage. Sometimes it is just ignorance or arrogance. Just an airtight alibi, weapon hiding in plain view, things like that. We'll check. Just to be sure. You know. Thorough. Relentless."

"Do what you believe you have to. I did not kill that witch, and neither did any of my weapons. But don't let me stop you. Test away. But I warn you, if you harm them in any way—if the patina is dulled, the speckling eroded or altered, fingerprints—I will come after you with the legions of hell." His voice is placid, but he sneers the threat and leans into it.

Jason looks right back, nods, and responds with a small smile. Jason notes that Flynn is so upset about the collection. Does he not realize there is more at stake than the collection? Jason ponders that as the smile eases.

When ballistics arrives, Atticus unlocks the cases. There is a subtle aroma that wafts from the cases. Oil, old metal, powder residue, a hundred hands. The techs take each weapon reverently off its perch and pack them up to take them all away.

Mason Oeillet dials his uncle's private number, braced for all hell to break loose. Maurice Oeillet is a wealthy financier, head of the massive Oeillet Empire—and a brilliant political manipulator. He personally directs the agendas of several PACs working at the federal level as well as wielding influence regionally and statewide.

The Oeillet family took up politics long ago, a sideline, the most important tendril of the empire. Each of the Oeillet grandsons knows a version of the history of the Black

Carnation. They know, for example, that their grandfather came from France by ship and endeavored to stake a claim in California, like so many others. They know that his methods were at best unconventional, and in the worst light, shady to criminal and perhaps even debaucherous on occasion. No one ever uses the terms *pimp, enslaver, traitor,* or *murderer.* On the other hand, words like *cunning, liar,* and *thief* are understood and, in an unspoken way, revered.

Great-Grandpa's colorful life is why the family stays out of the spotlight, at least off the *public* stage. They are all wealthy: insulated, legacy wealth. Their empire has continued to diversify and prosper over 150 years. Holding companies and land trusts, layers of documents hide them from view unless it is to accept some discrete recognition, some acknowledgment of their generosity in California in the twentieth century and into the new millennium.

There isn't a governor that they haven't influenced, and often unduly so, illegally to downright extortion. They put half of the governors in Sacramento. In fact, one of the first things Henry Junior did was move the family compound to the hills east of the capital, so their sphere was silently, subtly even more pervasive, in proximity if not in notoriety. Members of the family dabble in wine, art, and the performing arts. They are spread throughout middle California, from the bay to the foothills of the Sierras, to the North Bay.

The third Henry schooled his eldest son accordingly. "Maurice, the average politician may have a vision, good intentions, or even foolish inclinations. None of it matters if they do not have backers with clout. Politicians are really front men, or women. They must look good, play well, and turn a phrase to appeal to the public. The political stage is really all about attractive celebrity, not substance. They must look the part—and be able to talk the talk, not get frazzled."

"What does that mean?"

"It means blunt, brutally honest, straight talkers don't appeal to the public. Sincere truth is also unpopular. Politicians must be able to spin anything to sell. Do you grasp that?"

"I think so. But wouldn't people want to know the truth?"

"Well, they think they do. But, in reality, they don't want to hear ugly truth. What they really want is to have someone tell them what they are comfortable hearing and make it sound like the truth. And truth is sometimes a tricky thing. Sometimes a grain of truth twisted up to be palatable is more desirable than truth that conveys hideous reality. Reality can be frightening. A frightened public tends to react in ways that are destabilizing.

"That's where wealthy backers come in to play. That is politics in this state. The political climate is becoming more and more centralized into the hands of very few. We are the few, but the competitive field is growing and narrowing all at the same time."

"I don't understand, Father."

"Understand this. Anyone who seeks to lead the many must communicate with them. A politician can only travel to so many locations in a week, a year, a lifetime. But with a newspaper, over the radio, they can reach the many effectively. That is where we come in. We own the newspapers, radio, and now television. We are their voice. The question is to whom we lend our voice. We listen to their message, shape it and influence it."

"Father, what is the difference between influencing and telling them what to say? Is it right to tell them what to say?"

"Of course not on both counts. But we can present concepts to them and influence their visions of the future. That is as much our right as anyone else's right. We never mislead anyone. Sometimes it is as much about what we do not portray as it is what we do. We do not coerce anyone. We have the channels of communication. Others do not. And we can choose who we support just like everyone else. We have money. They need it. Do you understand?"

"You said that there were others."

"Yes. Yes. They are learning that politics in this state is what we make it out to be. They launch with seemingly noble ideas. But noble ideals rarely come along with comfort and ease. They typically mean hard choices and sacrifice.

"Unfortunately, Son, the public is a mass of people orbiting around a bell curve. Most of them are basically good people. And basically not all that bright. Most of them do not have the intellectual spectrum to understand how the entire world works and how even they themselves behave.

"They understand their family, their needs. They plan for a year, two. When they are young, they want to become players. They have noble ideas, energy. It is easy to inspire them. By the time they are thirty, they are probably married with a job, a couple of kids. By middle age, they start to think of growing old. So it is easy to encourage them. Tell any of them you will give them more than the other guy has to offer, and they will vote for you. Everyone wants more than they have. It is a powerful lever."

"But how do we give them those things?"

"It is not about the things that they get. It is more about their willingness to trade for what they want. Do you understand?"

"No. I don't understand."

"If I promise to give you what you want, if only you will trust me that I will find a way to pay for it, or to make someone else pay for it, and it will not impact you other than you will have more of what you want, will you trust me?"

"I would trust you, Father. Is there someone else to pay for the things they want?"

"There is always someone else to pay. It is also about control. If you rely upon me to give you everything you want, soon you will be less self-reliant. You will become dependent. Once they get those things, even if it isn't such a good idea in the long run, it met their need today. When it goes badly, they won't realize why, and there will always be someone there to blame. Someone—someone else."

"Why would someone do that?"

"Control. Everything in this world is about control."

"What you have been telling me, isn't that a form of control?"

"Yes. It is. And control is our ally, Son. Control in the hands of the masses is a bad thing. They don't really know what to do with it."

What Maurice heard was that it was a family duty to make sure that the right politicians were given a voice—for the sake of the people. And he set out to learn how best to serve the people, his trust. His trust and duty by birth. By the time the third Henry died, his son Maurice's empire was even larger. It included vast portfolios of ventures, all forms of entertainment and communication. And he had learned something else as well: power and control were really all that mattered. The true meaning of his father's words.

"I'm in a meeting, Mason, stepped out. This better be important."

"Appreciate it, Uncle Maurie. We got a situation up here. I need to fill you in."

"Can you give it to my assistant? Really—"

"Marie told me to call you. Sorry. We gotta talk!"

"Hold on."

Maurice came back on the line, having extracted himself from the meeting. "What's so important?"

"We got a nosy newspaper up here, and they are always digging up dirt on this and that. One of them dug up the Black Carnation." There was silence. "She has everything, his real name, the paper trail, places he owned, things he did... and she knows it's Great-Grandpa. She knows... everything. Old photographs, and I mean old. She's going to sell it to everyone. She wanted fifty million bucks."

"She would have taken less. I already know this lurid little tale. I have contacted people. It will be handled. And, Mason, I don't want to hear from you again on this topic or any other topic. Is that clear? Do you understand?"

Mason started to answer, then thought, *Marie! She mustn't have sold this all that well.* Mason feels awkward and alone.

Maurice Oeillet mutters inaudibly, "Dumbass!" as he returns to his meeting.

Lauren Riley stands at the door of the great wood-and-glass pinecone on the hillside. Ellie Skymyn opens the door and smiles richly to see her daughter standing there. "Toyá. I was hoping to see you. Better if you were actually here to see me, but I know that is not the case."

Toyá, the daughter, steps inside the pinecone and into the presence of the wisest person she has ever known. "Not this time." She moves to a comfortable location and sits down.

Ellie follows and does likewise. For a minute, they both look up through the glass to see the fallen snow, having fallen again off the steep shapes of the glass wedges. Some sky. Clouds. "Tea?"

The lieutenant takes off her jacket and sets it aside in the warmth of her mother's home, and responds, "Sure. Tea sounds great." Ellie goes to the stove and puts fire under the kettle. No microwave in this house. She prepares two cups that smell of herbs and berries. Settling in, smelling the twisting vapors as they rise on the steam, Ellie just waits for Lauren to speak.

"Mom, I have to ask you some questions."

"Figured. Glad they sent you."

"I sent myself. I'm lead on this. Well, my sheriff is here, but I am the lead investigator." Ellie nods, acknowledging that this is huge for her daughter and noting the duty belt. "And I need your help."

"If it is in my power to grant, I will give you anything."

"What's going on in this town, Mom?"

Ellie smiles, but it isn't derisive. She is accustomed to her daughter's directness and her complete lack of arrogance, her humility. "I believe you want to know about the casino."

"That's a great starting place."

"Our compact has been ratified as class III, and all we are doing now is waiting for the Moluku Council and Plumas County to clear the small stuff, like the environmental impact study, permits. They cannot stop us. They can delay us, and they can make our lives miserable—which they are attempting to do. But the courts are on our side."

"And you have the land, the money, right?"

"Yes."

"Then what is this with Atticus Flynn?"

"Really? He knows that the casino will half his kingdom, or worse. He is doing everything he can to delay, clinging to his monopoly on this town."

"He is not the only hotel, not the only restaurant, not the only entertainment in Moluku Lake. Surly others are also upset."

"True. But he is the biggest, loudest, the best, actually. What he has built is great. It put him on a throne. He rules. But he is corrupt. He gets away with murder in this town." Then Ellie realizes what she has said and laughs. "Not Logan Malloy. But if he had, and it was left to this town, he'd get away with it."

"You don't believe that."

"Yes, Toyá. I do. Do you not see how he struts through this village? How he believes he is in total control? He is charming, handsome—and I dare say, sexy. He has unlimited wealth. He expects to get his way and for people to placate his wishes. He expects cooperation. As such, he is the definition of arrogance and self-centered presumption. He's also manipulative, a master at pushing people's buttons. And if he doesn't get his way, he is vindictive and ruthless."

"Well, don't hold back, Mom." They both laugh. "So you do not believe Atticus killed Malloy. Or *had* her killed."

"Correct."

"What if I told you that Malloy was about to publish an expose on Atticus and his wife, Marie, and, well, the other side of Atticus. The fact that he is gay. That Jayden Listeri is his lover, or one of them. That Marie Flynn is nothing more than a beard."

Ellie smiled wryly. "Yes. I see that." Ellie pondered. "Then I'd probably say, 'So?'"

"You think Atticus would stand for that?"

"I bet it would really anger him! I bet he would be livid, and I bet he would have done almost anything to 'control' the situation, manage it to his advantage. Kill? No. Too much like actual work, too much risk. Just too much. Not at all his way of doing things."

"How would he 'manage' it?"

"By showing up with his wife on his arm, the perfect husband, brazen it out, laugh at the thought of it, shrug, and carry on. Demean it with apathy, not even deny it. He's too arrogant to cower or defend."

"That would work?"

"Years ago, someone tried to cast aspersions on Marie Flynn, suggesting that her family was actually a band of thieves or something. She wore an elegant single strand of white pearls and was amused at the idea of such a claim. It went away. They are like the Teflon Dons of the Sierras. Remember that. Nothing sticks to those people. But we are not mud, and we do not have aspersions to cast. We are real and inevitable."

"You didn't have a hand in this at all?"

"Well of course I did. Why not? I was hoping that Malloy would get him to back down, speed things up for us. Roger Haawim is nervous and wants this resolved. He is a good agent. It could have been the basis of brokering some deal to move things forward. I was hoping it might help. But she's dead, so on to the next strategy."

"So, who killed her, and what is your next strategy, Mom?"

"Ask yourself who else would suffer by Logan Malloy spreading scandal. And go see Elyse James at the newspaper. At the gala, she all but told me she had some new dirt, and I thought it might be on Atticus. She is beautiful, but foolish. She plays her cards too quickly, goes all in too often and too early. And as for the next strategy, well, time is on my side. But I might go talk to Elyse, too. You never know." Ellie and Lauren both smile. Lauren was very aware of her mother's ability to patiently move forward invisibly, almost imperceptibly, until the pieces were in their place. Sagacious old she-bear.

"Toyá, the Europeans have been a canker on the mountains for over two hundred and fifty years. I am patient like the earth herself. The People are not perfect. We made many mistakes and misunderstood many things. The Europeans will outsmart themselves. I do not have to worry. I may not live to see it, but they will pay a price for their greed and for their crimes against the People."

Lauren pauses for a couple of minutes. She allows her eyes to move across the horizon of her mother's great room, to see through the glass to the grounds surrounding the dome. Lauren lives in the world of the Europeans. It makes her nervous when her mother talks of threats to that world. Lauren is half European. She doesn't look European, but she got her height from her father, and she feels him in her.

"How can the Europeans pay a price? Who are the Europeans anymore? Aren't we all Americans? Not all of them had any hand in the things that happened. Many of them were not even here during the occupation, the gold rush. Some of them fought against the abuse, corruption, and greed. It is not a price that can be assigned. I think it is best to let old rocks lie where they land and move on."

"Toyá, that is because you think in terms of badges and courts. The price is not set by others. That is just vengeance. You must always ask, do I seek to change the world, or do I just seek to shift power? Even the People can get lost in this concept. Even the People sometimes seek retribution. It is a boomerang and can never resolve anything. Time is balance. In the end, it will be set by the scales of the universe.

There is a long moment of snow, sky, trees, silence, tea, and the smell of herbs and berries.

Toyá brings her dark, clear eyes to rest inside the gaze of Kapá, looking at her as if waiting for the inevitable. Kapá understands this struggle within her daughter.

Lieutenant Riley inhales and spits it out, "Did you have a hand in Malloy's murder?"

"No."

Betsy makes an excuse and leaves work. Her supervisor is surprised and not pleased. Extra guests, busy, but Betsy claims an emergency and departs. She goes directly to her babysitter's and picks up Katy. She intends to bring Katy to the café to keep her safe. On the way back, Betsy is forced to the side of a quiet road by two vehicles. One a sedan, the other a van. Betsy is frightened.

The tall man in the hooded parka gets out of the sedan and comes up to Betsy's window. He shows her that in his gloved hand is a small handgun pointing, not at Betsy, but at her daughter, Katy, in the rear car seat, who is curiously looking over to see what's going on.

"Thank you, Ms. Hall. We needed you to be the one to pick up your daughter." Now there is another man on the passenger side of the Escort. Another gun pointed at her. Betsy is shuddering inside. She has nowhere to go. She does not know what to do.

The tall man takes out a key fob and opens the locked car doors with the press of a button. The child is gone from the car seat in a flash. The second man disappears into the van and is gone. Betsy calls out, "No! No!" But no one is listening. Now she is sobbing.

"You see, Ms. Hall, we are in charge, and now you will do exactly as I told you in the restaurant. Is that not right, Ms. Hall?"

Stunned, tears in free flow, Betsy just stares back at the face, shadowed in the hooded parka. He also departs while Betsy's heart sinks, her breathing is stopped, and her mind races. She does not think to notice anything but the images of the gun, the doors opening, Katy calling, "Mamaaa..."

"The gun is clean, but the lands and grooves match—six narrow and, more importantly, the twist is left and stretched. This is the weapon. One of the beautiful old Colts. It is beautifully maintained. Everything is perfect."

"Yes. I saw them. Immaculate." Sheriff Noble thanks the lab, hangs up, and thinks of the gun collection. "We just gotta figure out who he paid and why he used his own gun," he thinks out loud.

"It was one of his guns, right?" Howard asks.

"Indeed it was."

"I've been wondering about the carnation, too. Why do you think, in her dying second, she grabbed a flower?"

Rodriguez remembers something Riley said, something he also remembers. "I don't know. It is odd. In a way, it is all odd. I mean, her house. It was austere. And then there's this vase full of carnations. At the scene, they were dead. The idea didn't stand out. But thinking about it they just don't fit at all."

10

SIGHTING MOVEMENT

Riley, following a hunch, calls Elyse James' cell phone number with no answer. She drives to Elyse's home, a cabin on the outskirts of Moluku Lake. Her car is not in the driveway. Riley knocks on the door, but there is no response. She looks in the porch window and sees that no one is visible; no movement. Knocks again, then several times. She goes to the enclosed carport and sees that there is a Lexus sedan, maybe four years old. She can see most of the license plate. Riley checks on her phone and verifies that it is the license plate of James' car.

Apparently, she is gone, but either she is on foot, or she did not leave in her own vehicle. Riley looks at the drive and around the cabin. There are no tracks other than her own. In fact, there is no disturbance in the fresh snow at all. No one has been here.

Riley calls the Moluku View, but there is only a recording and an emergency number. She dials it. "Greetings, this is Robert Shaw. If you are calling the emergency contact number for the Moluku View, please press 1. Otherwise, I am unable to take your call. Leave a message, and I will get back to you shortly. Have a pleasant day, and thanks for your continued support of the Moluku View!" Riley presses 1.

The call is forwarded and answers, "Robert Shaw here. How can I help you?"

"This is Butte County Lieutenant Lauren Riley. We were at your office yesterday, investigating the murder of Logan Malloy. I need to talk to Elyse James as soon as possible."

"Ah, yes. I remember you. Well, there is a production crew working at the paper, but they won't answer the mainline. I doubt Elyse will be in today, Sunday and all. Big night last night, you know. She is no doubt working on her piece about the gala, or she sent it last night and is sleeping in. You know how it is."

"Where would she be sleeping in? I am at her cabin, and she is not here, working or sleeping in. Her car is, but she is not."

"She probably took a cab or got a ride to the lodge last night. Doubt Elyse would drive her sedan in bad weather, dressed up, heels and all. She could have taken a room and stayed at the lodge. Digital age. She can do her work from anywhere."

"Did she file her story last night?"

"I don't know."

"Can you follow up on that, please?"

Riley drives to the lodge and inquires if Elyse James is a guest at the lodge. The answer is no. Riley asks if she is staying with another guest this morning.

"Impossible to say," the desk clerk responds with a tilt of his head and a coy half-smile. "I haven't seen her this morning, but we are very crowded. I can have her paged."

"Please."

Riley hears the page in the public areas. After fifteen minutes, the desk clerk returns to the lieutenant. "It is possible she is here and just not up and about yet."

Riley leaves an urgent message for James to call right away and exits the lodge. As she does so, she notices Betsy Hall go in the employee entrance. She is just about to turn the ignition when she has a thought. She returns to the lodge.

Betsy goes to the employee locker room and finds and puts on the uniform of a housemaid. She takes a passkey and empty laundry bin with her in the service elevator and up to the fifth floor. She turns the key in the lock of 533 and goes in.

Riley goes directly to the security office and requests the tapes from the gala the previous evening. She is given a download on a stick and heads back to the police department.

Almost an hour later, Betsy exits Room 533 and returns to the elevator. She and the laundry bin go down to the service dock, and she leaves the bin there and returns. She changes again and returns to Oeufs et Crème to resume her shift. Exactly as instructed.

Vianne returns to her home in Peregrine Hills from a passionate encounter with a virile companion half her age. The name of the young man is already fading from her mind, only the latest in a long line of discrete and well-paid companions. She comes in the back door of the home she shares with her husband.

Mason is in a club chair in the bar area. Vianne pauses, looks at Mason, and recognizes that he is still in the remnants of his tux, holding his cell phone. He looks like he has been beaten with a weary stick, the way he gets when he has drunk himself sober. Again.

"I see you had a big night."

"Apparently, so did you," Mason replies halfheartedly, seeing that Vianne is still in her gown with a topcoat cinched at the waist.

Vianne ignores the obvious. "It was good. Receipts were excellent. I think the Council can do just about anything on their list of projects."

Mason leaves it there. He no longer cares who Vianne spends her time with, last night or any night. He isn't interested in fidelity on either side of the equation. He does expect her to conduct whatever in a manner that diminishes the chance for him to be ridiculed in public or anywhere else. He rotates his head to gaze out into the great room. He is spent. He doesn't want to talk about last night. "I'm tired, Annie."

"Want something? Coffee? Breakfast? Shall I ask the cook to make something for you?"

She isn't sure why, but she suddenly feels a wave of compassion for this repulsive creature. She kicks off her heels and goes toward him. He throws his arms out and around her, pulling her in with his face pressed into her belly, nestling beneath her warm, heavy breasts. At first, she is startled, but she does not resist him. In fact, she folds around him in an uncharacteristic embrace. She cradles his fat head with her hands as he begins to sob.

Once, she had loved him. When they were young, he was impulsive, emotional, and did not behave like other young men, eager to prove they were tough. Mason was more available and spontaneous. She thought he loved her, too. Later she learned that his wealth and family—that could buy him anything, fix anything—made him thoughtless, reckless and boorish.

By the time she fell out of love with him, she was very much in love with the ease and options money could buy. They settled into more of a compact than a marriage. She would comply with what he wanted. She would live quite well. She would have a social position she could not imagine obtaining on her own and had no serious obligations... except showing up on Mason's arm when required and making no waves, for him or the family.

Of course, she had to put up with people wondering what she saw in him; Marie's obvious disdain. Marie.

Marie was married to Atticus, who was an arrogant ass, but he was gorgeous, charming, and sexually attractive. She would have done Atticus in a heartbeat, given the chance. But Atticus didn't give her the time of day and openly despised his brother-in-law. And vice versa.

Once in a while, she dances with Atticus, on this occasion or that. He is graceful, and his touch is gentle. Almost too gentle. Always the perfect gentleman. Always impeccably dressed. Smooth. She wonders what he would be like in bed. Often. She also knows that Mason is intensely envious of Atticus. So she is exceedingly careful.

She keeps her fantasies as part of her secret life, alone, by herself in the luxury of her bed, in the dark. There she is free to play whatever game she wants, with whomever she pleases to imagine. She slips into something skimpy and stands in front of her full-length mirror. Looking at herself turns her on. She is appealing. Loosen, reveal, even more turn-on. Touching herself really gets it going. A few cocktails, music, and some erotic toys, some that move or pinch, wet her. She has become accomplished at closing her eyes and pleasuring herself. It is part of her survival.

Here, in this moment with Mason, she is overcome by this display of vulnerability and curious as to what has precipitated it. When Mason doesn't get his way, he usually displays his rather explosive temper. But she has never seen him bawl.

She coaxes him upstairs, puts him in his bed, and goes to her own room to shower and get ready for a quiet, relaxing day. If all goes well, it will be by herself. If all goes well, she will spend a good deal of the day remembering what it was like to have someone strong, gorgeous, and relentless wreak havoc on her body in ways she would have otherwise had to imagine and often does. The day will doubtlessly end in play.

11

FOCUS OF GOLDEN EYES

Howard tries to reach Betsy. She must be working. So he goes to Oeufs et Crème to find her busy with a table. He gives her the high sign to break away so they can talk briefly, but she ignores him. He never intrudes on her life because he doesn't want to be obvious about his relationship with her—doesn't need the speculation, gossip. She is brisk in her movements. He notices because she is usually fluid, comfortable—genuine. His brow furrows for a moment, and then he decides to leave her alone. Find out later.

Howard goes to his office, walking into the conversation between Riley and Rodriguez. They are watching the security tapes from the gala.

"You were there last night, Chief Billings. Help us discern these people and their masks. Did you see Elyse James?"

"I did. She was there most of the evening."

"When did she leave? Or did she?"

"She was the slinky blue dress with the silver mask. Hard to miss her. I think I saw her last going out the big doors into the lobby, why?"

"I want to interview her and can't find her this morning. Not at her home."

"Probably stayed at the lodge."

"They were booked solid before the event—and not by her. So if she stayed, she stayed with someone else. Did she spend a lot of time with anyone in particular last night?"

"I think she spoke to just about everyone. No one in particular that I noticed."

"What time did you see her go into the lobby last?"

"Well, the band was packing up or gone. Midnight?"

"Kevin, main ballroom starting at eleven. At eleven, there were still a lot of people in the ballroom, considering the hour. But a lot of the masks were discarded. The band was playing their last set." Elyse, wearing her silver mask, is dancing with a man shorter than her. "Who is that guy?"

"That's one of the Art Council members. I think that's his wife over there, glaring," Howard points to the background capture.

When the music stops, Elyse goes to the bar and orders a shot of something, whiskey maybe.

In the background, on the dance floor, there is still a couple groping each other even though the music has stopped. A man touches Elyse's arm and speaks to her, but he is not looking at her face. He is clearly focused on what is just on the other side of that dress and hoping against the odds to get a feel, better a look. She turns and her eyes roll—even through the mask. Her appearance is provocative, she knows it, and she probably understands that at this point in the evening, any man unattached is hoping to hook up for some fun. Then she worked her way through the remaining guests toward the door.

"Lobby... at 11:50 forward."

Kevin clicks on the main lobby camera, and they begin watching. At 11:52, Elyse James enters the lobby and shakes one more set of hands. Chats. And still masked, heads, not to the coat check, but the opposite direction. As she disappears around the curve of the wall, they lose sight of her, obscured by a group of people sauntering through. "Where is she going?"

"She's heading toward the executive garage... and the private elevator."

Sure enough, just before midnight, the group of passersby out of the way, Elyse James, blue satin bag, barely captured, disappears into the private elevator. Riley tries the cell phone again. "Nothing. I have a hunch about this. I can't explain it. I'm going back to the lodge. Kevin, keep looking at the lobby and all the exits to see if James leaves the lodge. Officer, please go out to James' cabin and see if she has returned. Let me know right away one way or the other."

Lieutenant Riley arrives at the lodge and goes to coat check. Sure enough. Two coats have tags from last evening's event. One fur-trimmed leather. A man's. The other a full-length faux fur coat. Certain it belongs to Elyse James, Riley goes through the pockets: gloves (possible DNA), nothing else. She temporarily bags it in plastic and texts her forensic contact to pick it up. She heads to Eli Lucas' office straight away. "Mr. Lucas, sorry to intrude on your day, but I need to search the private floor. Again."

"Got a warrant, Lieutenant?"

"Not yet. But it is on the way, and in the meantime, I can freeze traffic to or from that floor. And I am doing so right now."

When Riley arrives on the fifth floor, most of the doors are open, and housekeeping is busy stripping beds, vacuuming, and cleaning. "I want this to stop right now," she speaks, pushing from her diaphragm. "Please stop what you are doing and leave everything right where it is. Please stop. Thank you. Please turn that off. Thank you. Please move into the hallway and remain there." The four doors that remain closed eventually open with guests in various stages of readiness, peering out to see what the ruckus is about. That is all Riley needs. "Good afternoon. I am sorry to disturb you, but we are conducting a murder investigation. I am going to need your names." Murmuring, shuffling. "Please provide them to this officer. Thank you."

Eli is beside himself, trying to soothe his guests and remain calm himself.

Elyse James is not on the fifth floor.

"You have no right, no warrant—"

"Here it is," she interrupts, slapping it into Eli's hands, not eager to take it.

"I have tried to cooperate with you, but this is outrageous. Do you know who these people are?"

"I don't care. I had probable cause."

"What cause? You lost track of an individual at the gala? That is nothing. You can't do this!"

"We'll see. Elyse James never left this lodge last night. She is here somewhere, and I am going to find her." But underneath, Riley is a bit unnerved. After all, there is no trace that Elyse James was on the fifth floor of Eagle's Nest. And yet, Riley knows that she was there.

Howard catches up with Betsy as she arrives at her apartment. He lets her get inside before he approaches the building. Then, straight to her apartment. She doesn't expect him, and she is more rattled by his entrance than he would have expected.

"I haven't got time right now, Howard."

"Katy's not here, right. At the sitter? We got time."

"No. I've got things to do. You need to go."

He tries to fold her in his arms, longing to feel her press into him, but she averts his reach and reiterates, "I said 'no!'"

"What's wrong, honey?"

"I got some things I gotta work out. By myself."

"Tell me what's going on. Maybe I can help."

"No, you cannot. In fact, you make it worse. PLEASE, Howard. If you care about me, just go away for now."

Howard is alarmed. He looks at her, but she does not make eye contact with him. Should he press her or trust her? He decides on the latter. He kisses her; she turns her cheek to him. He is confused, worried, but leaves.

But he does not leave anything behind. He takes every image, word, and movement away with him in his mind, and he knows that this is trouble. He decides to stay and keep an eye on things in his cruiser. But then his radio goes off, and he reluctantly heads back to the lodge.

"She could have come up and then left again," the sheriff offers.

"She is nowhere on camera. How did she get out? And why is her coat here? She did not leave here, last night, in that dress."

"I don't know, but she is not on the fifth floor. Got that guest list for the fifth floor?" the sheriff queried.

"It's in the warrant. So we will have it soon." Riley feels like she is standing on a dock, one foot on a drifting boat, as the call ends.

She is determined. "Everyone who was here last night gets grilled. She had to be somewhere on this floor, and somebody knows it because she was not in a room by herself! Someone has to have seen something, know something!" Riley states. "No one who is still here leaves until interviewed."

She sees Chief Billings exit the elevator. "Chief, I need someone to go over those recordings and map every single entrance and exit to this lodge since midnight—staff, cigarette breaks, guests, attendees, the works! No exceptions! And I need to contact everyone who stayed on this floor last night."

The chief shakes his head but initiates the work, only half in this world. His other world is out of control, he knows nothing, and there is nothing he can do. He heads to the security office to get more downloads. He assigns one of his officers to sit in the security office and take over one of the monitors there. He gets a list of the cameras from the guard on duty and heads back to the department to get as many bodies on this as he can pull in, on or off duty. Back behind all of that, he worries.

"Lauren, why are you so jacked up with this?" the sheriff inquired over the phone. He had gone down to his office to check on things with his undersheriff and captains. "I get that it is a mystery, but we got a murder to solve. We don't know that she isn't snug up in some getaway with a guy. Besides, we know it is all about Flynn. I think we should be focusing on him."

"Think whatever you want. But Elyse James did not file her story about the gala last night or this morning. And I went to meet with Ellie Skymyn this morning."

"Ellie Skymyn *Riley*, right? Your mother." He is gratified to hear this.

"Yes. Along with a lot of other things, she told me I should talk to Elyse James. Then, when I try to do that, James has disappeared."

"Why did she want you to talk to James?"

"She wasn't sure, but she thought James knew something. James said something at the gala last night that implied my mom should listen to what she had to say. The gala wasn't the right time or place."

"Too bad she didn't make it the right time and place."

"Regardless, THIS is wrong, and I know it. Something is wrong, and I believe it is connected to the murder. She knew something. So did Logan Malloy. Malloy's dead, and Elyse is missing. I think it is the hinge of this whole affair."

"OK. We'll make it hang together. By the way, we were talking, and that carnation is starting to really bug me. Rodriguez said that after thinking about it the vase of flowers doesn't seem to fit with Logan Malloy. Said you had made a comment about the place. Austere, I think he said."

"Yes. Unadorned, to say the least. I get it. So why is there a giant bouquet of flowers? Huh."

"Well, anyway, Eli Lucas is upset, and that means his lawyers have descended on our office to protest the disruption. They're making all manners of threats, but the truth is, I gave them a copy of the warrant that you *finally* got, and, at least for now, the court is buying probable cause based on making James a material witness and her apparent disappearance. It's thin. I suggest you find her. One way or the other. And I hope to God she has the goods. Otherwise, we gotta get our focus back on Flynn!"

"I understand," she says. But Riley doesn't understand what is going on. What she does get is the void, the skip in the beat and the disconnect. Her brain tells her that she is risking her entire career and position, right in front of her sheriff, on a hunch.

Intellectually, she is aware that it makes more sense to behave more equivocally. She knows that. She is objective. This calls for objectivity. The murder weapon. James. They don't fit. Go with the sure thing! Logic says to get Flynn and grill him till he breaks. She also believes she is right about this hunch. She pauses for a moment and lets it all swarm over her. Carnations? Nothing fits. She decides to inch out a little farther on her hunch.

12

STALKING SKY

Riley heads to the James cabin yet again with a warrant and a forensic team. Inside, they search everywhere, and they take the computer, any discs, and flash drives—anything and everything.

Standing in the middle of the bedroom, looking around at the furniture, the possessions, she is reminded of looking around Logan Malloy's great room. Elyse is not spartan. Her cabin is cluttered with probably second-hand, upscale everything. Elyse was more insecure, reaching to be what she was not.

Riley's eyes land on a photograph of Elyse James. She replays the phone conversation with James that first day. She realizes she never got the chance to meet James. "She is beautiful," she thinks to herself and recognizes a hunger in the eyes. She recalls Elyse's tone during that conversation, the flippant coyness. *"Perhaps I just wouldn't tell you HOW I knew if I did. It's our sources that we guard most jealously."* "Sources," Riley repeats out loud, *"I'm not inclined to keep secrets if they are juicy.* "You enjoy secrets, exposing them *'as it suits you,'"* Riley says to herself. "To whom would you expose a really big secret, and why?" Riley remembers that

Elyse James was keeping something that first day, something. Riley is pondering, "Elyse enjoys games, but Ellie says she may not be that good at them yet." Riley wonders if she has overplayed a hand in this risk-laced community of conspirators.

They complete their search, taking whatever is deemed relevant, including impounding the Lexus. Riley is in the closet and randomly picks up a boot that catches her eye. She's not sure why. She turns it over to look at the sole, and there is a tiny fleck of something. Dirty white, cream, maybe. She bags the pair. Inside a small case on the closet floor, beneath two shoe boxes, Riley finds a single small flash drive with the initials "LM." She takes it.

Howard knocks softly on the door, and Betsy opens it. She is quiet and does not make eye contact. Howard takes her in his arms. She does not resist this time. He holds her. He is grateful for being invited in but still disturbed by the unusual reticence to look at him. "Where's Katy?" he whispers.

"She's sleeping."

"What happened today, honey?"

"I don't want to talk about anything. Can't you just hold me? Make me feel safe?"

"Always. Anytime." As he says it, he realizes he means it. So he holds her close. And with a new urgency. Earlier, when she had pushed him away, he had felt a quake inside. It lasted until just now. It begins to dawn on him how much this woman matters to him, and the idea of losing her has become unacceptable. *"That is going to be a problem,"* he scolds himself.

"There's a lot of stuff on this drive. On a lot of people besides Atticus Flynn. Photographs, documents, notes."

"But this file, here. 'Oeillet.' It is in a file all by itself, and it is a big file."

"What's in it?"

"Research. Old, old photographs, names, downloads. Humm. It's all about this notorious criminal. Here, look at this—it is an old sketch, a wanted poster. Reward for information as to the true identity of 'the Black Carnation.' The file name is Oeillet."

"Carnation? Carnation. Carnation!" Riley exclaimed quietly.

"Damn!" the sheriff exclaims equally quietly.

"It's about the Oeillet family. It's not about Atticus at all. Maybe they were fighting about this. Maybe Elyse killed Logan to get this file? Took the thumb drive to bury it, steal it, write it herself?"

Sheriff Noble thinks for a second, eyes to the right and down. "How about this? Elyse took the drive to use as blackmail or extortion? I like that version. Elyse James sees this as the biggest story the Moluku View has ever broken. She wants to run it, but Logan Malloy is intent on torpedoing Atticus Flynn."

"People just love to see the powerful fall."

"And they love to see the lily-white perfect people exposed as flawed!"

"Elyse is tired of being in the shadow of Malloy, they fight, Elyse has a plan to make her big career move. They fight, Malloy winds up dead, and Elyse has the drive but hasn't used it yet. After all, she is barely starting as the big cheese."

"It could work. But if so, where is she? Why didn't she file her story? And how did she get Atticus' colt?"

"Yes, all troublesome loose strings that don't seem to tie." They both ponder.

"Maybe she is out roping in an even bigger catch. Maybe she is in Sacramento?"

"Without her car?"

"That guy, what's his name? Shaw."

"Yes. Robert Shaw."

"Didn't he say that she wouldn't want to drive her car in all the snow?"

"All dressed up. She wouldn't be dressed up to go to Sacramento. But that gives me a thought. What was she wearing on that tape?" Riley questions.

"Oh, I can recall it clearly. Barely-there blue thing hanging from tiny straps."

"I don't recall seeing that dress at her cabin." Riley calls down to the lab to verify that it isn't in the inventory, wasn't in the closet, and not in the photos. "She never left the fifth floor, and she never arrived home."

The sheriff smiled. He felt for the first time that they were onto something with this. "That is very good, Riley."

"Thanks."

"Where would she go with a hot secret?"

"Up to the fifth floor to spring it on someone. But who?"

"Got the list? Who all was on the fifth floor that night?"

"Well, one member of the Oeillet family was in 533, Mason Oeillet," Riley replied.

"Bet it wasn't with Mrs. Oeillet."

"Nope," says Riley. "We saw her leave by herself early in the morning, and she never went into the private elevator."

"That old letch was doing Elyse James." Sheriff Noble recalls Mason Oeillet storming into his office, insisting that

Atticus Flynn had murdered Malloy—or had it done." He ponders what an ass the mayor is and begins to form a pleasurable scenario where he watches that blow-hard get cuffed and walked out. Of course, that meant foregoing Atticus in cuffs. "Oh well, life is full of trade-offs," he tells himself.

"And what about the murder weapon?"

"Honestly, I am not sure how that fits in, yet. But I know this is right!"

The sheriff knows she is correct. The fact that the colt somehow ties it all back to Flynn adds anticipated gratification to the prospects.

"Shall I go talk to Oeillet?"

"No. Let's send a car to bring him in for questioning. No cuffs. Yet."

Marie Flynn is seated on the chaise in her private sitting room, pondering recent events. Her imagination is formulating the more desirable scenario where the eager beaver reporter had killed her brother. How much better that would have been. She doesn't bother to rebuke herself. In fact, she would have considered paying for her defense. "Too obvious." Marie switches the crossing of her legs. "He has always been a fool. Not a single wit. In his defense, he's the first-born male child of the generation. All deference, of course," she says to herself facetiously.

Knock, knock, and Atticus enters with a vase of fresh carnations. "I presume your event was as successful as it was spectacular."

"Yes. Successful." She pulls herself back from distraction. She has always buried her resentment of Atticus' carnation boutonnieres and vases of carnations. "Thank you. I appreciate you being at these occasions."

"My pleasure. I enjoy the tuxedo events," he said, adjusting a flower in the vase.

"No one does it better." She smiles.

"This Logan Malloy business is a bit tricky." He places the vase auspiciously on a table and adjusts one more flower.

She is annoyed but does not display even a ripple. "Really? How's that?"

"Well, they are trying to pin it on me," he says glibly with a slight tilt of his head back and feigned laugh. "Fortunately, of course, I have an iron-clad alibi. So I think they are getting weary of dragging every twist and turn to my door."

"Well. Did you kill her?"

"No. Although I am delighted that someone did. When they discover who actually did it, remind me to send them roses, champagne, caviar, and a check for their defense."

Marie recalls her recent thoughts and smiles. "Yes. Well, I have not observed anyone grieving. If all goes well, it will be the end of that horrid publication—the Moluku View. A more appropriate name for it would have been the *"muck view."*

"It is good for business. Malloy stirred up this and that, and the next thing is everyone coming out to see what's up and who's down. You know, without that rag, we'd all just sit in on cold nights and read a book." Atticus feigned laughter again.

Marie did not laugh. There was an almost imperceptible shake of her head and a small squinting of the eyes that might pass to the casual observer as the hint of a smile.

"I'm going to run into the lodge and make sure everything is bouncing back. By the way, another trip is on the horizon. Europe. I'll give Ms. Brody the details so she can get started. What are you up to, my dear?"

"I have correspondence. I'll stay in."

When Mason Oeillet arrived at the police station, he was met by the family attorney, who walked in with him. "I have a message for you from your uncle. Don't say a word unless you are given permission to speak. Then, 'yes' or 'no' is advised. Understood?"

They were escorted into an interview room where Deputies Riley and Rodriguez were waiting. Jason Noble was in the audit room.

Without a word, they pressed the playback on the tablet and showed Mason Oeillet the shot of the ballroom entrance, Elyse standing there; Mason arrives and briefly touches her hand. "What did you say to her, Mr. Oeillet?"

The attorney nods, "I don't recall."

"Looks like you took her hand. Actually, it looks like you passed her something. What was it?"

"I think I congratulated her. Promotion at the paper. I greeted a lot of people that night, as did we all. That was the idea. So what?"

"So, we cannot locate Elyse James today. We are questioning anyone who might know where we can find her. How about you? Know where she is?

"No."

Another keyboard hit and the shot of Elyse's bag disappearing onto the private elevator played. "She went up to the fifth floor, Mr. Oeillet."

"So?"

"We were wondering if you ran into her on the fifth floor. We got a shot of you going up there, and actually, you registered in Room 533 that night. So did you happen to see her?"

"No."

"Later the next day, we were at her cabin. Searched it, too. Didn't find much. Didn't find that snazzy dress she was wearing either. Odd, don't you think?"

Mason shrugs. The attorney doesn't move or flinch.

Riley interjects for the first time, "We did find one thing. This thumb drive. It was hidden in her closet."

Mason's foot begins shaking under the table. It is only noticeable in the slightest vibration that is perceptible to someone right next to him or a trained and sensitive observer.

Riley continues, "You know what was on that drive? Research, old photographs, records, and a story. An interesting story."

Mason turns his head slightly to look toward the lawyer, who simply places his hand on the back of Mason's chair. It is a move anyone might make. It is intended as reassurance, calming.

"Turns out, it is a history of the Oeillet family, its origins, and it makes some rather remarkable claims. The sort of claims that might be unwelcomed by such a respectable, influential family. You're a member of that respectable and influential family, Mr. Oeillet. She didn't happen to share any of this with you, did she?"

The attorney speaks, "Of course, since you put it that way, we will need to see your warrant and the details of how you obtained that drive."

"You don't need to see anything. Your client needs to answer the question."

"My advice to him would be to understand the nature of what you are implying before answering any further questions. Perhaps Ms. James could answer that question for you. My client will not."

"Then we will hold him here while we continue to search for Ms. James."

"Grounds?"

"Material witness in a disappearance of another witness in a murder investigation."

"That won't last any longer than the court in Plumas opening in the morning. Unless I can get a judge on the phone tonight."

"Stand up, Mr. Oeillet." Riley proceeds to read as Rodriguez puts on the bracelets.

As they exit the interview room, so does Sheriff Noble from the audit room. Mason loses all composure, "Son of a bitch! What the hell do you think you are doing? I'll—" He is cut off by a firm yank on his arm by the attorney.

"Shut up! And keep it shut until morning. I'll see you then."

The attorney escorts Mason down the hall. Then he steps outside the precinct for a moment and makes an urgent phone call to Sacramento.

Betsy cannot sleep. She does the unthinkable for the second time in a matter of days. She dials Howard's cell phone. He answers. He is not asleep either. "I'm in trouble. Please help me."

Howard tells his wife that he has to go into the office, pulling on pants, boots, and a jacket. Betsy has never called him, except for the morning she found Logan Malloy and this call, in the middle of the night. He knows it is bad.

Betsy is huddled on her sofa in her robe and wrapped in a throw. She is crying quietly but profusely. "Yesterday, a tall, thin man came to one of my tables at the café. He told me to do something. I didn't want to do it. He threatened Katy. Then he left. I made an excuse and left work to go get Katy." Her eyes are searching Howard's for encouragement. She is not sure this is smart, but it is imperative. She can contain herself no longer. "That is just what they knew I'd do."

"Who? Who knew?"

"I don't know. Please just listen. They stopped me on the road and took Katy out of my car at gunpoint. The tall, thin man told me that he would harm her if I didn't do exactly as he had told me at the café." Betsy pauses, her brow furrowing with a question that keeps plaguing her. "The doors opened. Somehow."

"What? Wait. What had he told you?"

She paused. Terrified. Not sure what she is neck-deep in, she is not sure what will unfold once she explains. But she also knows she cannot be silent. "He told me to go up to the fifth floor, into 533, and to clean up."

"And did you?"

She nods. Pauses. Takes a breath. "Howard, there was a body in there. That beautiful reporter. She was dead. Strangled, I think. Naked. I did as I was told. I put everything in the laundry bin. I cleaned up. Wiped down every surface, vacuumed and scrubbed the bathroom. I changed the bed, towels—everything."

"Blood?" Howard interjected.

"No. But it was horrible. I was so frightened." She searches his face, looking for the judgment she fears. "Then I took everything in the bin down the hall into the service elevator and out to the loading dock. I left the bin there just as I was told. And I went back to my job." She is still searching but finds nothing but alarm and concern.

Howard knew that this was the monstrous thing that the lieutenant was hunting. He reached out and pulled Betsy into him and held her. He knew that her life was going to be a nightmare. She was coerced, but she was coerced into becoming an accessory after the fact to a murder. He knew that his life would never be the same, probably ruined, because he also knew that he would stand by Betsy, come what may.

Howard drove her to the police station, and they entered quietly through the back entrance. He placed her in his office and went to get Jason Noble.

Vianne Oeillet does not know where to go. She received a call from the *family* attorney's office, an attorney she has never heard of before, explaining that she is to refuse to discuss anything with the police, or basically anyone else for that matter. She was told that there was a problem and that *it* might get rough for a while but that she and Mason would be taken care of and fine as long as she just stays out of it. She was given a number to call if she needed anything. She dials Marie.

Marie isn't in the mood to talk to Vianne, but she also realizes it might be in her best interest to keep an eye on her. "Yes, Annie."

"The police came and took Mason to the station for questioning, and I got a call from the family attorney's office telling me to keep my mouth shut and not talk to anyone. Mason has not returned."

"Then why are you talking to me?"

"I don't know what else to do. What is going on, Marie?"

"I'm sure I don't know, but everyone is being questioned with regard to this unfortunate murder investigation. They came here that first morning. I had nothing to tell them. Just do as you are advised. Go about your business, and don't talk to anyone."

"Mason was upset. After the event. *Upset.* He was here at the house when I arrived. He was upset in a way I have never seen before. Not like that. I am worried. Do you think Mason is mixed up in the murder?"

"Do you?"

"He can be an idiot. He doesn't always think a thing through."

"Doesn't always?"

"I think he had business dealings with Logan Malloy. What if he lost his temper and did something horrible?"

"Then you will have to trust and listen to the lawyers. Take a deep breath, Annie."

After listening to Betsy Hall, Jason Noble and his two deputies pulled up the camera on the loading dock. Sure enough, there was Betsy rolling the bin out to dock. It did not trigger any notice earlier. She is dressed like housekeeping, rolling one laundry bin onto that dock. Maybe a little early by the time stamp. But nothing unusual. It did not take long for an unmarked van to roll up to the dock, and a driver loaded Betsy's bin into the van. No one had even noticed. But there it was. Simple as that.

Jason knows they were dealing with clever people. The man did not kidnap the daughter. Betsy picked her up from the sitter. They did not go up to the fifth floor. Betsy did. There is just that truck and a guy in a parka, hood, and cap that had a bill and flaps over his ears. Virtually no shot of his face. They could approximate height. The license plate in the back has mud on it, so it is virtually unreadable. Good one. The angle coming into the dock was obscured, so no shot at the front plate. Make and model. That is all they had. That and Betsy's story.

Betsy is holding her daughter, sleeping in her arms. She is rocking and imagining her life wrecked, wondering what will become of Katy. Would they come back and hurt Katy? Who are they? Her mind is racing, but she is also numb. She is treading in two separate realities. One where this nightmare is unfolding. The other, her dreams and aspirations, her daughter, the life she had just a week ago. She cannot get them to sync. She cannot get her brain to engage in anything but churning thoughts. She cannot make her body feel, yet she is so tired, so very tired.

Howard comes into the room and kneels down next to Betsy. He takes her hand holding Katy as she rocks. He sees her face, the fear, the turmoil, and a numb stare. She is not crying, yet tears are cascading down her cheeks. He wants to reassure her, but he knows that for a while, things are going to be rough. He puts his hands gently on her upper arms, "Hey." She looks at him. He smiles right into her eyes, into her soul. "Betsy, I need you to be as strong as you can be. We need to find this guy and stop him."

Betsy nods.

"I want you to be very brave and work with a sketch artist. We need to know what the man in the hooded parka looks like. I know you don't want to think about it."

"I didn't get a good look at him because his face was always in the shadow of his hood." Yet, when she closes her eyes, she sees his face, some parts of it, piercing her, frightening her. "I will try."

At about 1 a.m., the phone rings in the squad room at the Moluku Lake Police Station. Riley had asked one of the officers to drive the bagged boots directly to the lab in BC. She had begged to get them examined immediately. Someone had done so. They are calling with information, for Riley. The sole of one of the boots not only has a crushed petal of a carnation, but it also has minute traces of blood.

"Thank you very much!" No DNA yet, of course. Riley is absolutely certain it will prove to be Logan Malloy's blood.

The next morning, Mason Oeillet was no longer a material witness, and his incarceration no longer centered on Logan Malloy. He and his lawyer were presented with an arrest warrant in the disappearance of and likely death of Elyse James.

"Habeas corpus."

"Your client stayed the night in Room 533. This morning, before the cleaning crew hit the fifth floor, our witness saw Elyse James dead in that room."

"My client will admit to being in that room but left it early in the morning. Someone else could have entered that room, someone already on the fifth floor, entered it *with* Elyse James, and killed her in that room."

"That is not what happened, and you know it, Mason!"

"My client left that room at 2 a.m. and swears that he was alone at the time. What is the time of death?"

"We don't have it yet. But when we do, it will prove that she was dead before Mason left that room," Jason says with a straight face, not a flinch or a breath out of sync. Riley watched with a new appreciation for her sheriff's ability to bluff a weak hand.

"I think we will have our own examiner take a look at the body. We will establish our own time of death if you don't mind." The lawyer played the bluff right back to the sheriff, calm, without a flinch or skip of a beat. The two men held each other's eyes, and they both let a couple beats go by.

"Fine. We'll get back to you on that. But for now, we'll hold onto Mason."

"See you at the arraignment, Sheriff, and I assure you, it will be expedited."

The lawyer left with his client down the hall. "Nice play, sir, but that won't work for long. Especially if they had anything to do with the disappearance of the body. We better find that van, the driver, something."

Rodriguez added, "How many cameras are there in town that we can find the van on after it picked up the laundry bin?"

Howard answered, "There are seven cameras along the main road. I'll get someone on it. That's good. If we can at least know which way it headed, it would help."

"We haven't opened the road yet. They are here somewhere."

"Well, Sheriff, if I wanted out of this town, even now, I could make my way out, trust me," Howard countered. "But a stranger, maybe not. You'd really have to know the lay of the land. That and everything is buried in snow." Then he thought, "Wouldn't hurt to have eyes in the hills, especially the east foothills. I'll call Sheriff Wade. He will have experience and deputies he can spare.

Chief Billing's small police department is stretched and tasked to the hilt covering all the angles on this murder. Most have slept little over the past few days. Howard is tired. No sleep. Added to this, suddenly, it is all about Betsy. She is in trouble, and Howard is no longer on the sidelines, wanting to insert himself into the solution and ensure that Betsy is freed from it.

Yet, more than ever, it is essential that he does not compromise himself. Particularly since his affair can no longer be concealed. He is looking at the ruination of his career, the breakup of his family, and his list of dishonors exposed. But he only cares about getting Betsy out of this mess. He only cares that she and her daughter are safe and have their lives. It is dawning on him that he is in love for the first time in his life. Howard calls the Placer County Sheriff.

In the interview room, the sheriff has pulled Riley and Rodriguez aside, "Right now, we have no proof that Betsy Hall is not in on the whole thing. She could have been paid off. We should check her bank account and talk to the daughter. If she confirms the abduction, then we can clear Hall," Sheriff Noble states.

"Do you think she is lying?" Rodriguez queries.

"No. But I think we need to get confirmation." Jason knows that he needs to do that for the case's sake but also for Howard.

"Hate to grill the daughter, but ask her a bunch of questions. If it is all true, she's gotta be traumatized. We should do it as informally as possible," Riley said, looking at the two men.

"OK. Do it without Howard Billings present. While he's busy. Just Betsy and the daughter. Only."

Betsy is still in Howard Billings' office, holding her daughter, who is sleeping. Betsy appears to be dozing, or at least trying to. The office door opens, and Riley and Rodriguez enter, trying not to disturb, but Betsy snaps to awareness as the door opens, and she does not speak.

Rodriguez crosses and kneels down low in front of Betsy, whispering, "How are you doing?"

"OK. Tired."

"I'll bet you are. We need to talk to Katy. Is that OK?"

"She is sleeping."

"I know. But it is critical that we ask her a few questions. We need her to confirm what happened yesterday. You understand."

"I told her not to tell anyone. I was afraid."

"Was she upset when she was returned?"

"She hugged me. Tight. She was confused. I told her that I had to do something and that the men were helping me. She did not believe me. That hurt worse than anything. She knew I was lying. I didn't know how to tell her the truth. I didn't know what to say. Please don't upset her."

"Perhaps we can help her to understand and recognize that you did what you did under stress to protect her. But we got to hear what she has to say. She may have information we need. We wouldn't do this if it were not necessary."

Betsy looks long and deep into Kevin Rodriguez's eyes. She does not want her daughter involved in this any deeper, and she sure doesn't want her to become a witness in court or a trial. She also does not want to live in a world where such men exist and might reappear in their lives. She knows there is much more at stake than confirming her story. She is sure of that from looking at Deputy Rodriguez. "OK."

Katy is awake, if not alert. She opens her eyes and glances up at her mother. Katy looks at Deputy Rodriguez. "Katy, do you remember driving with your mother away from the sitter's house yesterday?" The child answered with a nod. "Do you remember what happened while you were driving?" She nodded again. "Can you tell me what happened?" Riley brings in milk and some cookies and sets them on the table.

Katy looked up at her mother, uncertain. Betsy smiled and said, "It's OK to tell the deputy. Tell him exactly what happened."

Riley is in the background, leaning on the wall, observing. She sees no deception. She sees fear. And she sees that her partner is good with the child, and the mother, for that matter. She decides that he will carry this interview forward and she deliberately in the background, recognizing that the child did not need complication or distraction.

"What happened, Katy?"

"I can't tell, or they will hurt my mom."

"No one is going to hurt your mom. They just said that to frighten you." Kevin reached out and placed just his fingertips on Katy's arm gently. "If you can tell me what you know, we can catch these men and make sure they don't harm you or your mother. Just tell me what you remember."

"The car went off the road?"

"Imagine that was scary." To which Katy nods. "Then what happened?"

"Two men took me out of the car, and one of them put me in a van and drove away. I didn't want to go. I cried, and he told me to shut up, or they would hurt my mom."

"Did you see a gun?" Katy nods slowly. "Tell me about the van."

"It was empty."

"What do you mean it was empty?"

"There was nothing behind the seats. It was just empty."

"Where did the man take you?"

"I don't know. He gave me a dog to hold."

"A dog? A real dog?"

"No. It was soft. White."

"A plush toy. Did you leave Moluku Lake?"

"I don't know. He put sunglasses on me, but they were blacked out, so I couldn't see anything."

"OK. How long did the car go before it stopped? Like ten minutes, half-hour, longer?"

"I don't remember."

"OK. Tell me about when it stopped."

"I had to potty. I told the man. He didn't stop for a long time. Then I told him I would have to potty right now, so he stopped on the road, and I peed in the snow, and I didn't wipe."

"He didn't stop for a long time. How long?"

"It seemed like a long time. I had to potty."

"Did he let you out, or did you get out?

"He let me out. And he watched."

"Was he wearing a coat?"

"Yes."

"What color was it?"

"It was dirty. It was dirty white, like the van."

"Good. Did he have on a hat?"

"Yes. And a hood."

Carefully, Deputy Kevin Rodriguez leads Katy toward a description of the man and the van, every scrap she could recall. Lauren smiled at his patience and how clever he was to let Katy tell a story rather than respond to an inquisition. But it did not help. There were so many places for the driver to pull over that it was not feasible to try to find the spot.

Then Katy volunteered the single most important piece of information. "Then he gave me to another man in a car. We drove for a long time, too."

"What man?"

"The first man. The tall man with the hood."

Kevin says, "You're doing great, Katy," and unwraps the cookies.

Outside the room, "We got the van. Left town to the east further into the mountains. Probably heading for 395. But it was much later than when Katy was in the van."

"That's OK. I think we are piecing this together. The van went back to get the laundry bin. They were passing the kid back and forth, driving so they weren't spotted anywhere. Stay on the van. If they can get to 395, there'll be a camera in Bishop at least—if they get that far. Call Wade. Stop that van."

The sketch based on Betsy's description is on the table in front of them.

Lieutenant Riley believes that the noose is ready to cinch and goes to Howard Billings with a new direction. "Discretely place a watch just outside the Flynn Mansion, front and back. Then pick up Willard Dawson and bring him in, but leave the watch there. I don't want any one of them or their vehicles taking a ride right now."

Sheriff Noble winks at Riley, "Time to talk to the tall, thin man in the hood."

13

FLYING INTO THE STORM

Mrs. Flynn rang the doorbell with a kid-gloved finger of her left hand. Her right held her matching kid clutch purse.

She waited. When Logan Malloy opened the door, Marie watched as Malloy stood there for just a moment in self-indulgent satisfaction. Malloy was dressed in only her nightclothes and heels. The sheer draping of the gown left nothing for Marie to conjure regarding her breasts, waist, and hips, and the kimono was slipped off her shoulder, so the sight was vulgar but stimulating. Marie felt a gripping in her belly, but it dissipated as Marie imagined that this creature was in a moment of great triumph. Doubtlessly a moment she had dreamed of for a long time.

The moment passed, and the creature spoke, ever so barely slurred. She was drunk. "I've been expecting you. Please come in."

She calculated Malloy was celebrating, and it annoyed her that Malloy felt gratification in her arrival. Unfortunately, it could not be avoided. She entered the impressive split-level home and followed Malloy down into the great room, where a small fire warmed the space. Logan had a platter of cheese and fruit laid out on the coffee table. She was drinking what appeared to be a martini and offered a glass of wine to Marie from a bottle sitting uncorked on the table. She poured. Marie did not take it.

Without looking directly at them, Mrs. Flynn observed the vase, full of white carnations, as background to this meet. Noted but refusing any reaction, "What exactly is it that you want?" Mrs. Flynn inquired.

"Exactly? Right now? I want your husband to suffer the loss of his throne. His financial hold over this resort. I want to watch him twist in the wind as that casino takes prominence, devours his business, and, more importantly, his unbridled tyranny."

"Atticus Flynn has made this village the hottest spot on the mountain. Everyone here, including you, are what you are because of him and his magnificent lodge. And you begrudge him basking in his own domain?"

"He is deceitful, maybe even villainous. He gets away with it because no one dares to cross him."

"Jealousy, is it?"

"I wouldn't call it jealousy. I would call it a hostile takeover on a social plane."

"My," she scoffed. "Call it whatever you like. You want to dethrone him, push him aside to increase your own power base in this 'resort.'"

"Sure. OK. Whatever. My motive is irrelevant. That I can do it, is. I can't wait to see him squirm. I actually believe that you, Marie, will also enjoy that." Again, the personal reference. Mrs. Flynn's face ever so slightly tightened, her eyes a tad more squinty. Otherwise, she did not flinch. "I can't believe that you don't harbor at least some resentment."

"I don't. I have always known who and what Atticus is. He has always kept his side of the bargain, and I, mine. What gall you have to imagine yourself a champion of righteousness. It is you who poisons this community. It is you who should be devoured and then spit back out. You create nothing. You build nothing. You are nothing but a horrid little gossip. A parasite."

"Interesting that you should mention poison, Marie." Mrs. Flynn resented that this little viper elevated herself to first names. "Speaking of poison, I've been doing research into the ignoble past of the thirty-first state. You know, in the history of the wild, wild west, few places had the horrifying origins that the gold rush ignited. The two decades that followed the Sutter Mill incident really beg to be told. Kidnaping, torture, murder, extortion, sexual servitude, and debaucheries that few of the states could equal. Talk about genocide. What some people did to the indigenous people has barely risen to the surface, let alone noticed." Logan drank down the last of her martini and poured another. "There were a lot of bad guys back then. After the gold, the land, the power. Imagine my surprise when I came across one of yours. What was his name again, Bouche?"

Mrs. Flynn allows her focus to move to the large cut glass vase filled with dozens of white carnations. She realized that Atticus was not the quarry. She had underestimated the nature of this ambush. She steeled herself to remain as ice in the cold: strengthened by degree and shaped by the force. She said not a word.

Logan Malloy continued with thinly-veiled glee to articulate the legend of the infamous *Black Carnation*. How he terrorized the foothills, raided entire villages, cheated, stole, and murdered his way to wealth and power, then vanished. "Some said he returned to France. Others said he was himself murdered—by a vengeful Indian, brother of a maiden ruined. Some say the maiden ultimately died of syphilis. Probably more than one of those. So, there could have been a number of unforgiving brothers, fathers..." Malloy paused and smiled, looking Mrs. Flynn directly in her left eye. "But you and I both know that is not what happened."

Mrs. Flynn did not react in any way visible or measurable.

"Bouche, the debaucherous villain, took great pains and carefully, meticulously reinvented himself as the banker, the financier, Henry Oeillet. He married the beautiful daughter of Angelo DePaschi—who, by the way, was no saint. I have an old photograph of her. Actually, you look a lot like your great-grandmother, Marie. Or is she your great, great... well, irrelevant detail."

"So, it isn't Atticus and his empire you are after."

"Oh, I want that, too. But you are correct. Atticus Flynn is just the appetizer. It's you, Marie. I want you to live out your years with everyone seeing through the pearls, the soft leather gloves." Malloy gestured toward her adversary, observed that Marie still had them on, still clutching her purse. Frozen.

"What does a mealybug like you want more materially than the ruination of your foes?"

"Oh, Marie, even you do not have that much money. You have no idea how much I desire, long for you to lose everything you value—your haughtiness, your immaculate throne, your superiority, your smug indifference to everything you deem beneath you. That is what I want, and it has no price tag. Your family cannot fix this. You cannot fix this. You can just prepare to face your comeuppance. You will see how quickly all those people, your crowd, will turn on you and relish your demise."

"You believe they will care?"

"Well, not for long, but they will never look at you the same. You will never sit upon your marble throne again. They will see you for what you are. The daughter of sociopaths, with bloody hands and rather impressive manipulative skills. That's all, darling. Just scum like the rest of us."

She paused her lecture and brought her inebriated eyes to focus on Marie. Behind the icy eyes, Malloy saw a bright, piercing light. She thought it to be cold light, like the sun through ice and fog. She didn't realize the magnitude of her miscalculation. Malloy turned to face the plate glass window to let it all settle in on Mrs. Flynn. Savoring the moment.

Marie Oeillet Flynn stood like a glacier for a moment, pausing like almost frozen water sliding down an ice cycle. Then, smoothly, reached into her kidskin purse, withdrew Atticus' single-action revolver, and cocked the hammer, at which point Logan Malloy turned into her last ever surprise.

Marie Oeillet Flynn stood with her arm outstretched, slightly elevated, pointed directly at the beating heart of the venomous little viper, and pulled the trigger. She watched with pleasure as Logan grappled with the shock, the effects of the bullet. She wanted it to hurt and enjoyed the creature's flounder and fall. She heard the sound of the weapon dissipate and heard the wind outside. She relished the moment when the gusts of wind overcame the fractured window, and she listened intently to each cascading piece of shattered glass rain down on the last seconds of Logan Malloy's life. But all contained within her stately pose. She did not even look up to the open window and barely noticed the fire flare with the oxygen and then flicker in the sudden temperature drop. Marie stood above the open eyes now looking up at her, a gasp, fear. She enjoyed looking down her cheeks, knowing that her image was imprinted upon this impertinent wretch's brain.

The wind was whipping, already lapping up moisture and turning it into tiny crystalline structures. The fire flared again and then began to smolder. "Time to go. Ta-ta, now."

Mrs. Flynn exited the front door, got into Atticus' Range Rover, and backed out, as she had come, scrunching her own tire tracks, without headlights, onto the road, turned, and drove away as snow was falling. She missed the Lexus parked without headlights up the road in the opposite direction. Marie was enjoying the world, somehow cleaner now. If not cleaner, it was certainly more orderly. She ignored the fact that her world was far more complicated.

Atticus would be home by now, tired, unaware that the Rover was missing. He would have no alibi to explain why his prize antique had just killed his arch enemy. The only one who would possibly miss her was the butler, Mr. Dawson. No one could be more loyal to the Oeillet family than Willard Dawson.

The suspects would be endless. Atticus at the top of the list. Either they would not be able to find enough clues to definitely prove any one of them did it, or if they did, it would all lead to Atticus. She hadn't touched anything. Her entire body was enclosed and covered, save her face, but the fur on her coat would catch any skin cell that might have fallen. She had carefully wiped her feet before entering—the courteous thing to do under any circumstance. She smiled.

Logan had been right about many things. Marie not only resents her husband but finds his private behavior and his choices vulgar. She smiled at the idea of her pompous husband as a lovely accessory. She laughed a little out loud. He was handsome, elegant. He was a charming and an enviable escort: useful, but not essential. She finds it amusing to see women flirt with him; his flirting back, polite encouragement, yet aloof, taunting, and cruel—all so amusing.

Marie could survive his ignominy. But the truth about the Black Carnation? Not so easily. It would not sit well with the Oeillets at all. It would not work harmoniously with decades of manipulation from the wings, to be suddenly thrust into the spotlight of infamy.

But she didn't do it for the sake of the family. Marie is 62, older than Atticus by four years. She, a beautiful young girl, had grown sophisticated and accustomed to the indulgent and forbearing world she had created for herself. She enjoyed the role of the empress of Moluku Lake. She had worked diligently at building her throne, just as Atticus had his. It did not occur to her that she had no qualifications to merit her rule in a more competitive environment. She was content with her tiny empire in the mountains. For decades, she had held herself apart from her repulsive brother—no small challenge. She was not interested in a tarnish or erosion at this late date. Unlike Maurice Bouche, she was not interested in reinventing herself.

It was not easy to be an Oeillet. She had endured the family's focus on politics. Although she lived an insulated life as a result of their wealth and influence, she also believed the distastefulness of political machination was beneath her.

Inside the frigid palace of her being, Marie was trying to find the words to explain her behavior to herself. It was not like her to take rash action and certainly not to be introspective. She left for Malloy's with Atticus' revolver. Clearly, it had occurred to her to put an end to that troublesome woman. "That bitch!" As the words escaped her lips, decades of stifled passion rose to the surface for her to examine. For just a brief moment, Marie realized that she hated the prison of her life; she did not love it. She felt a furry to flee. Then, with practiced agility, she closed it off and resumed her ride home, in the cold, using the subtle shivers and shudders to re-lace her persona. As she did, she decided it was beneficial to have a little brigand in the blood.

Once the Range Rover was out of sight, the Lexus pulled into the drive at the Malloy estate.

Willard Dawson sits in the interrogation room, tall and poised. Sheriff Noble, Riley, Rodriguez, and Chief Billings watch him from the audit room. "I wonder if he will be so dignified when we show him the sketch." Billings questions.

"Humm. Let him sit for a while. Got to be curious, nervous. Practiced veneer," Riley says.

"Military."

The sheriff tosses his file open in front of Riley. Sergeant Major Willard Paul Dawson had gone to Vietnam on March 8, 1965, as a private with 3,500 US Marines at Da Nang. He was not an advisor or a trainer. He was there to advance the military resistance to what was perceived to be an expansion of communist interests in Southeast Asia. He distinguished himself through four tours and was promoted in the field with a flourish of citations for his sense of duty and diligence, as well as his operational accomplishments.

Beyond that, he seems almost invisible and obscure. Driver's license, taxes, no marriage of record, not even a parking ticket: clean as a whistle.

What the record does not tell was once he returned home, he found employment with a private security company, hired most often to protect businesses and families who had concerns about dissident organizations like the Symbionese Liberation Army. The small company was also the action arm of a large, family-owned conglomerate known at the time as Corsican Enterprises. There he found favor for his sense of duty and diligence and found his way to more interesting, comfortable, and trusted forms of service.

It was an hour before the sheriff went in and sat down across from the butler. "Missed you yesterday when I visited the estate. Went there to check out the gun collection. But you were nowhere to be found. Some sort of butler errands?"

"Yes."

"What errands do butlers run these days?"

"Aside from personal errands, business for the house."

"Yesterday personal or business?"

"I'm not sure that is any business of yours."

"I assure you it is my business. What kind of business did you have yesterday?" Dawson sits silent and calmly looks at the sheriff. "OK. I think I can jog your memory. Seems you were in town and keeping some pretty shady company. We have witnesses that saw you, in a parka, with the hood shading your face, but not so much that they couldn't provide a description of the tall, thin, older man who looked like this." He lays the sketch on the table in front of the butler and just waits.

The butler is not in a hurry to look at the sketch but condescended to do so by simply lowering his gaze and then re-elevating it to meet Jason's eyes. He says nothing.

"No comment?"

"It is just a sketch. It means nothing. Someone's description. An artist's interpretation of that description."

"Yes. But we also have you on camera in the lodge at the same time as two witnesses claim you were there; talking to one of the waitresses. Then you left and got in a car that is similar to one at the estate. A sedan." Jason plops down the image taken from the camera in Oeufs et Crème.

"That could be anyone at all."

"Kidnapping a child at gunpoint, extortion, aiding and abetting murder, obstruction of justice, tampering with evidence, not to mention the murders of Logan Malloy and Elyse James. That's what we are talking here."

That does get a small reaction: an inhale and a lift of eyebrows, and the dignified chin. Then an exhale, a squint of the eyes. "I have nothing to say, Sheriff, nothing whatsoever."

"You drove the Range Rover to Logan Malloy's house on Friday night. You had taken the 45-colt pistol from the glass case where it is kept. You murdered Logan Malloy. No one thinks for one minute you did it for yourself, Dawson. We know you did it for your employer, Atticus Flynn."

With that, the veneer opens to reveal a delighted smile, no teeth, just a broad, smug smile and a distinct twinkle of the eye. But not a word.

The sheriff continues to look Dawson in the eye for a minute and then gets up and leaves the room.

"I don't think that should have amused him. His disdain was huge, and suddenly, he is laughing at me?" Jason looks around at his fellows, and then it hits him. "He knows we got it wrong! Let me see that file!" Jason looks at Dawson's file, and it clicks. "Check out Corsican Enterprises! Oh my god! That's it! He worked for the Oeillet family before he worked for Atticus Flynn. Atticus Flynn. Dawson doesn't work for Flynn. He works for the lady of the house. He works for Marie Oeillet Flynn! Riley, come with me!"

Mrs. Marie Oeillet Flynn sits in an upholstered, armless chair in the gun room. A pale blue wool dress, simple lines, and a single string of pearls. She is wearing off white shoes, her kid gloves on, and her matching clutch purse in her lap. Her gloved hands are folded on top of the clutch purse. She is smiling, but her eyes are cold. "Please come in, Sheriff.

Lieutenant," she nodded toward Riley as if to get credit for remembering. "Sit down, won't you. Would you care for tea, coffee?" gesturing toward a small sofa opposite where she sits.

"Thank you, ma'am, but we'll stand."

"Of course. I suppose you have some questions."

"I think maybe we should take a ride to the station and talk there if you don't mind."

"But I do. I think we can talk fine here, in Atticus' gun room, don't you? Really, it is appropriate, wouldn't you agree?"

The sheriff looks around the room at the glass cases, empty of their elegant old revolvers. He says, "We can talk here if you prefer, for now. Where does your husband keep his keys to the cases, Mrs. Flynn?"

"He keeps them on his personal key ring. There is another set in the gun safe."

"Can you open the gun safe for me, Mrs. Flynn?"

Marie smiles, a one-sided smile as if only half of her being sees the humor in that question. "It's always something obvious, isn't it? Combinations. So the individual can remember, thinking no one else would ever guess what obvious thing has been selected. Dates usually, right? Birthdays, anniversaries, old addresses, or phone numbers. The date my husband met Jayden Listeri was 06202015. One or two tries is all it took.

"You're probably wondering how I could remember a date like that. I'm sure Atticus thought the same. But you see, the minute I laid eyes on the young, beautiful, ambitious Jayden, I knew who he was, what he would do to our lives, and how Atticus would be used by him, and he by Atticus. I remember it very clearly. Atticus is like the sun, glorious, blazing in space and with massive gravity. He draws in everything, good and bad. Everything orbits him, warmed or burned by his light and energy."

"So you did love him."

"No. I wanted him like someone wants the Hope Diamond. It is just a diamond, large, but really, diamonds are a dime a dozen—if there were a free market. But as it is, the Hope is rare, blue, valuable, and all its owners are cursed. Did you know that?" She smiles. "They say if you shine a light on it, it will glow after the light is turned off. That is Atticus. He has his own fire.

"He shows well. Can you understand that? When someone has everything they might want, when life is perfect, one turns to obscene accessories—cars, jewels, trophy wives, extraordinary things, because they blaze..." and as if she caught herself on some other plane, she abruptly returned to the conversation. "No one could love Atticus. With all his flash and fire, he can appear so warm if he elects to, but inside, he is ruthless and cold. He does not love anything or anyone but himself."

"And Jayden?" Riley asks.

"Atticus wanted him. He is gorgeous. And ambitious. Jayden wants a career. A really big career. The caliber of career that needs help and a few steppingstones. It was sealed the minute they met."

"Did you always know? About Atticus?"

"Of course. In the day, it was not uncommon. Gay men took wives. And they are charming in a way that other men are not. So women took gay men. They are attentive and enviable without... messy expectations. And Atticus was discrete. He traveled. Out of town, you understand. Not so much of late."

"If you knew and you don't love him, why not just divorce him? Especially after Jayden showed up?"

"What would be the point of that?"

As Marie talks, another kind of light becomes visible to her audience, listening, absorbing and comprehending. "Why did you do it?" the sheriff asks.

"I already told you. I have everything I ever wanted. My life is perfect. I even have the Hope Diamond, and everyone envies me for it." She shifts slightly in her pose. Her eyes survey the room. She blinks a couple times as if clearing her vision of something. "I don't want to weather one more storm. I don't want to be impervious to it all anymore. Consider inevitable permeation. Perhaps the rain finally found a way in."

"Logan was the rain?"

"Let us not place credit where none is due. She was an odious insect that needed to be swatted."

"But not, I would think, by someone like you, Mrs. Flynn."

"I was delighted to take care of it. Civic duty and all." Mrs. Flynn pauses, smiling with a muffled chuckle. "Decades of poise. Containment. Maybe I am tired. Maybe I hate it all as much as I love it, but I could not let it go, just as I cannot escape!" Then, she smiles. It broadens to a grin, but a tear glistens in her eye. She holds the tears at bay, trapped in surface tension, an inhale. She would not allow that!

Marie's hand moves swiftly, uncovering the small handgun sheathed in the purse, up to her throat, aiming at her brain. The small weapon fires before Riley can think or act.

They both stand, captured in the moment, transfixed. Eleven heartbeats, echoing the sound of that shot before Jason can move his eyes to the brains and blood splattered on the empty glass cases.

Riley recovers first and steps toward Marie's slumped body since fallen on the floor. She squats beside the dead woman. Most of the left cranium was missing. The smell of gun powder and warm blood, coppery, wafted. The right side of the face fairly intact, cheek, the valley between it, and the nose wet with freed saline, tears spilling at last. "'Small handgun.' What do you want to wager Betsy will recognize it?"

Snapping back into the room, Jason replies, "Small pistol, large bore. Wow. I'll call it in."

14

TALON GRIP

"Do we tell him, or no?" Riley questions.

"Better question—what do we tell him?" the sheriff replies.

"OK. We could have Rodriguez tell him we've gone to pick up his boss. See what he says or does."

"If we were waiting for a confession that would be the way, for sure. But we know 'his boss' killed Malloy, all he can do is fill in some details. But Elyse James. That's what we want to know."

"I say, tell him. Just see what he does."

Noble nods and they exit and enter the interrogation room where Willard Dawson sits, still tall but a little less posed. Tired, maybe? Riley hopes that some of that aloof dignity is wearing thin. "We have bad news, Mr. Dawson. Marie Flynn is dead."

Dawson looks dully for a moment, as if waking from some trance. As if the individuals entering the small room were not worthy of his attention. The words don't penetrate right at first, then his head cranks slightly to the left, and his brow furrows just a bit. "I'm sorry, what did you just say?"

"I said that your boss, Marie Oeillet Flynn, is dead. She killed Logan Malloy and didn't want to suffer the state the price of a trial," Riley repeats, monitoring the sarcasm, wanting to sting a bit but not wound.

Dawson's face drains of color, and his features slacken; his gaze moves to the top of the table, but his mind is calculating. Then he looks up, "You are just saying that to get a rise out of me."

"I am sorry, but she put a small pistol to her throat and blew her brains all over the gun room. She's gone. You are alone. But she left you something to remember her by—you will be charged with complicity, at least after the fact, in the murder of Logan Malloy. More interestingly, you are complicit after the fact in the murder of Elyse James. Want to tell us about that?"

He doesn't speak. His eyes move from the lieutenant to the sheriff and back again. Measuring. As he does, his face shows more emotion than in all the time prior to this moment. He forms a snarl that melts into pain. Denial appears in the form of stiffening of the jaw and the mouth. Then tears fill the reservoir of his eye sockets, but a tiny jerk of his head chokes them off. His shoulders slump, his head bows slightly, and his gaze falls to the table once again. But he still does not speak.

Noble and Riley just wait. Interviewing is part procedural, part drama, and a large part the ability to read the subject: know when they have something to tell, when they won't, and when they will. And, more importantly, when they want to and when they need to.

When Dawson lifts his head, his eyes, he also rolls back his shoulders, and the Sergeant Major reappears, self-assured and confident in his record, his service, and his loyalty. "She was magnificent. Ms. Oeillet. She was beautiful, intelligent, such elegance and grace. She never should have married that fop! He does not deserve her! I hoped she would get rid of him a long time ago. But she... she kept him. She kept the pretense, the sham of that..." His voice trails off, and he struggles for the strong veneer. Pulls it up once more. "She knew she could count on me. I was always there for her. When her father died, her uncle sent me to look after her. I could not believe my good fortune, to be sent, to be paid, to be with her, in her house, her confidant. But you know, she never complained. That was beneath her. She was so solid, so composed and intractable. I served under officers who did not have her equilibrium, her bearing."

Riley and Noble are leaning in, actively listening, encouraging with empathy, compelling Dawson to unburden himself.

"I saw her leave the house that night, in the storm. I knew she was undertaking an extraordinary mission. But I didn't know. Until I went into the gun room and noticed one empty case." He looks at both of them. "When she returned, I did not want to create any complication for her. I stayed in the shadows. She went into the gun room, opened the safe, took out the kit and cleaned the weapon, replaced it, returned the kit, and closed the safe. Then she calmly went upstairs. The limousine did not arrive for several hours."

"And Elyse James?"

"Her brother is another animal altogether. From his teens, he was undisciplined and began to feel the boundless options that were available to him. Instead of establishing focus, he squandered the possibilities of the life that could have been his. I had no respect for him.

"He got away with murder..." he hears what he has said and grins on one side of his mouth, "—per se, and accomplished nothing. He was ultimately a great disappointment to his family and eventually showed up here to strut around in her world, soiling everything he touched.

"And then, he actually did murder someone and expected to get away with that as well. And who does he come to for help? To my mistress, to Ms. Oeillet. Ms. Oeillet just wanted to clean up the situation in that suite. It was the family that sent the cleaners to take care of everything else. My job was to get that waitress to clear out the room. That's all. And I did, and I didn't do it for the idiot brother! I did it for Ms. Oeillet. I did it for... Marie."

They pause for a moment, hearing the personal reference, recognizing that this old soldier is faithful and unrequited. Then Riley asks, "The family. How do you know it was the family, Willard?" extending the personal reference.

"Because it was the family fixer that called me on my cell phone. I told him that I could take care of the room. They said I would be contacted by some people who would do the rest."

"And this is in your cell phone. Right?"

"Yes. All in my cell phone."

"Do you think they knew about Malloy?"

"No. Well, everyone knows she's dead."

"What makes you think they didn't know about Ms. Oeillet and Malloy?"

"I just do. They didn't."

They leave the interrogation room and Dawson to his grief, joining Rodriguez and Billings in the audit room.

"Well, well," Rodriguez says, eyebrow raising as he smiles.

"Indeed," replies the sheriff, "that cell phone will link us to the dispatch of that van and probably who was driving it."

"We already dumped the cell," Billings adds. "That's enough to start."

"Then the trick is to get to that body as quickly as possible!"

"Well, it's not going to be easy. That family is gargantuanly powerful in ways that we can't even imagine. If we squeeze them, they will squeeze back. So it's not over yet. Now the real political battle is about to engage," Sheriff Noble interjects. "I think we have to help them see that cutting their losses as far out on this limb as possible, as early as possible, is the smart thing before the rot can get anywhere near the trunk."

"It might be better if it does get to the trunk."

"Justice on that plane may be overdue, but it is also above our pay grade. Our mission is to close these murders, and the best way to do that is—at least for now—sever this branch from that power. I'll start working on that," Sheriff Noble says. "I have a smart friend in a fairly high place. I'll consult with him first. Put the old soldier on suicide watch and tell me where Mason Oeillet is right now!"

Mason's attorney doesn't need any advice regarding the family's interests. He is dutiful, diligent, and insistent in getting the nephew of his boss out of detention. It takes a five-million-dollar bond, a tapestry of strings, and one severely bent arm. As he prepares to depart, the attorney tells Oeillet three things. "Mason, you need to know that your sister is dead."

"What?!"

"Yes. Apparently, suicide." Mason's mind alternates between blank and blinding images. Of all the possible outcomes, that is not thinkable. He is grappling with the words when the attorney continues, "Also, the Flynn family butler is in custody and being questioned." Mason hears this with a sharp intake of air along with a gripping in his chest and sickening in his belly.

"And finally, Mason, a message from your Uncle Merle. We draw a line here. You have become an intolerable liability, and the family interests cannot be infringed upon, let alone damaged by this lurid situation. Do you understand?"

"I am an Oeillet! You can't push me around! Intolerable? Who do you think you are?"

The attorney's polish stiffens. He is confident he knows exactly who he is. His head tilts slightly back, and his chin rises just a tad so that he is looking downward as he continues. "Yes. Intolerable. Do not call your uncle or attempt to communicate with him in any way." Mason feels his chest in deflation, and the next breath is painful. "If you comply, a reasonable fund will be placed at your disposal that may allow you to navigate your way out of this *situation* as best as you are able."

Mason imagines what he is saying might be true. "I'm being cut off? You can't cut me off! I am an Oeillet!" he flounders.

"What you are is a beneficiary of a trust. Nothing more. And as such, you are subject to the terms and conditions of the Trust from which you benefit. Now, if you fail to comply or drag the Oeillet family into this *situation*, no funds will be offered, and your family interests will be cut off in accordance with the Trust. Is that clear?" The attorney does not await an answer, opens the Hummer door, exits the vehicle, walks to the idling limousine, gets in, and it drives away.

Mason is barely aware of the departure. For the first time in Mason Oeillet's life, he feels fear. Not the shallow fear, not passing fear, and not irrational fear. His heart seizes a beat, literally paining him. He is operating on panic reflexes, but his body is unresponsive. He does not know what to do. He thinks of calling his uncle, but the words replay in his fractured mind, *"Do not call your uncle or attempt to communicate with him in any way."* Heartbeat, beat, beat... "Marie!" It begins to settle on him more definitively. "Marie is dead."

He sits motionless. When his brain engages again, it is to feel the vulnerability of being out in the open, downtown, people everywhere. He wants to be safe. He wants to disappear. He can't go home. He needs to think. He begins to add up what he has been told beyond the finality of Marie and the castration from the family. The butler, Marie's butler. He knows everything. With Marie gone, there is no one to protect him. He will blab. He has no cards to play. "Neither do I," he thinks out loud. Marie would know what to do.

It does not occur to Mason that Marie was able to calculate the situation quite accurately, and she did know what to do, the only solution that afforded any autonomy of will or action. Marie was always self-contained and purposeful. It was unthinkable for her to place herself into the influence or control of anyone else or to imagine them dictating any moment of her existence. Mason has lived his life reacting to just about everything and has had no purpose whatsoever.

It also does not occur to Mason that this intervention is perceived by some as an opportunity. An opportunity for him to choose to be autonomous and make his own decisions as well.

Instead, without Marie to intercede or tell him what to do, he is a flounder. He thinks of where he could apply pressure, get some traction. He realizes he has more enemies than friends, and it occurs to him that all his blustering amounts to little without his family to back him up. He feels small. He thinks of seeking help from a friend, only to realize, for the first time in his life, he actually has none. Not one.

On the other hand, who all knows what has happened? Really. Maybe he can get to someone who he can still pressure or bluff. No one leaps to the forefront of his mental ramblings. An insane concept enters his frayed mind. He turns his Hummer toward the east shore of the lake, first forcing his way through the congestion in the downtown area, then heading north on the main road.

"He got released on a bond and left the station about an hour ago."

"Damn!" Sheriff Noble was not expecting the Oeillet's to work that fast or efficiently. He collects himself. "I'll worry about how the hell that happened later! Right now, put an APB on him and anything he might be driving. Meanwhile, everyone check anywhere he is likely to go. I want him back here immediately!" Sheriff Noble is not happy.

"Someone is already on the way to his house," the chief says.

"He won't go there."

"City Hall, maybe?"

"I think his instinct will be to run. He's a sniveler, a worm, so he'll try to go underground," Riley states.

"The roads are still closed," Rodriguez says.

"In and out of town. But he can get up in the hills."

"If the weather clears, we can get a bird up to find him," the sheriff says.

"In the hills, he has to have a place to go, or he will run out of road and have to hoof it. I don't see Mason Oeillet trudging through the snow."

"He has a Hummer."

"Yes. But owning one and knowing how to handle one are two different things. I already have a picture of him nose-diving into a ditch or demonstrating how many times that big box can roll over, dealing with gravity, out of control!"

"I'll give you that," accompanied by restrained laughter.

"We've contacted the City Council, and none of them have seen him."

"He doesn't seem to be at the lodge."

"Get Lucas on the phone. I want to know if there are any other secret rooms, panels, floors, or anything else at that lodge or anywhere else in this freaking town!" Sheriff Noble was reacting part from disbelief that they had let Oeillet go, and now he is in the wind and part from urgency to get a very disturbed and desperate lunatic contained.

When Atticus shows up at the lodge, Eli decides it is an opportunity for him to leave a little early. It has been a stressful week, and Eli is ready for extra time at home to recuperate. He makes a few last checks on this and that and heads towards Grace.

Eli Lucas is at home when Sheriff Noble locates him. Grace is listening to Eli's end of the conversation as she prepares take-out, brought from town, planning an intimate early dinner for her and Eli.

"We are looking for Mason Oeillet, and I need to know of anywhere you might think he would go if he was desperate and in trouble."

"Well, he wouldn't come to us. He is no friend of Eagle's Nest. We are unlikely to provide any shelter for him." Eli is amused at both the call and the implications of it.

"Perhaps. But you are the keeper of secrets in this town. If there is something you can tell me about where he might go, it would be appreciated."

"Believe me when I tell you that I would not hide anything from you, Sheriff."

"You have."

Grace snuggles into Eli's torso supportively. "That was different. It was my responsibility to protect my partner. I have no interest in protecting Mason Oeillet or any of the conspirators in the casino crowd. As far as I am concerned, you can pack them all out of here, the mayor, the Indians, and anyone else involved in that casino deal. I'd help if I could!"

Grace interjects. "You know, Mason was just downtown with that obnoxious Hummer bullying his way through traffic, honking, running lights..."

The sheriff overhears what she says. "Put your wife on the phone, Eli." When Grace takes the phone, the sheriff says calmly, "Where exactly did you see Mason Oeillet?"

"Right downtown. You can't miss him in that beastly thing he drives—"

Sheriff interrupts, "Which direction was he headed, Mrs. Lucas?"

"Well, let's see, he was driving on Main Street heading in the opposite direction of Peregrine Hills—"

The sheriff interrupts again, "How long ago was that?"

"Why, half an hour ago, less than an hour..."

"Thank you, ma'am." Sheriff Noble hangs up and turns to his team.

"He's heading to the east shore."

"That is basically rural residential. There is nothing over there."

"It is sparse. Lots of open land. Maybe he plans to walk out."

"No. He wouldn't do that. It'll be getting dark soon."

"OK, teams to East Shore, including canines, and get me a weather forecast, now!"

Riley is adding this all up in her mind. She heard the conversation with Eli Lucas and Grace. "No. Couldn't be! He wouldn't be driving erratically to meander out of town. He's going somewhere. Somewhere on the east shore. Something else," she tells herself. But she cannot think of anything else.

She isn't moving. Sheriff notices, pauses, and looks at her.

"Sheriff, Lucas said that Eagle's Nest was no friend to Mason Oeillet."

"Yes. Clearly. Are you saying I shouldn't have called Lucas? What is it, Lieutenant?" He recognizes her stance, a tone in her voice.

"No. Actually, that call may be the key. Eagle's Nest is on the opposite side of the casino's interest, right?"

"Yes. Of course...?"

"And the opposition is, the casino is the Maidu."

Billings jumped in, following, "Oh yeah! I saw Ellie Skymyn talking to Mason at the ball. Talking, like business, like allies."

"Are Wade's guys up there?"

"Probably by now they are."

"Let them know to be on the lookout for that H2!"

No longer reacting, they were in motion like trained soldiers with their orders.

Kapá stands at her kitchen sink, finishing a small mountain of dishes. She does not own a dishwasher, and she does not use a dish drainer. Instead, she washes the skillets, the pots, each dish, cup, and glass by hand; rinses, dries, and puts them away on their shelf or hangs them on their hook.

She sees it as time allowed to herself, to be one with all around her: the trees and things that grow from the ground, the rocks and stones, the deer, coyote, the burrowing creatures, and those that soar in the air. Kapá is grateful. Humbled by it. She allows the thought of it all to fill her being until it expands beyond her body; and takes in everything, the rivers, sky, mountains, and an infinity of stars. The bones of her ancestors and all humans who have walked Earth. She feels infinite and small at the same time, and her heart fills with gratitude and joy. For the moment, it is quiet. She has these moments. Gifts.

She opens her eyes, turns to the kettle, and fills it with water. Her water comes from the creek fed by a spring on her property. She sets the kettle on the stove with a low flame, and she thinks about the idea of property. A thought her great-grandmother could not have even conceived. Kapá smiles. She sees the oversized vehicle driving from the road toward her pinecone. Although the sun is behind the western mountains, it does not have its headlight on yet. She watches patiently, waiting.

She crosses to the door, opens it, and steps out on the threshold just outside the door. She watches Mason Oeillet descend and clumsily make his way through the crunched path that leads to the door in the growing shadows. "Come in, Mason. I will make you a cup of tea."

"I don't drink tea. But I'll take something stronger."

"You'll take the tea. It is all I have to offer you, and it will do you good. Warm you up."

He is torn between a need to seek her help and a desire to tell her this is really all her fault. "OK. Tea. For now."

Mason is intimidated at the thought of entering the home of this councilwoman. But to his surprise, he is welcomed by the warmth, aromas, and simplicity. He is in unfamiliar territory on many levels. He isn't sure how to approach the subject. He sips the tea. It is hot. He sets it down.

"It has been an eventful few days, Mason," she takes the initiative.

"Yes. Not much good has happened."

"Things may be difficult, but they are perfect just as they are unfolding. Why are you here?" And just like that, she brings it to the brink. It is her way.

"I need your help. I'm in some trouble. And I was thinking that—"

"You think that because we had business dealings, perhaps we will help you now. Is that it?"

"Well, yes. I mean, I got into this mess trying to help you—"

"I don't want to kick you when you are already down, Mason, but the truth is that you may have tried to help, but fundamentally, you didn't accomplish anything, and now you've made a... mess. Your word, right? Do you want to tell me about the mess?"

"Not really. What I can say is that I'm in over my head and need a way out, bad! Time. I need to be away for a little while. I need to think."

"What about your 'connections,' Mason. You are well connected on your own. You don't need our help."

He picks up the cup. Sips. Stalling. Reaching for words that just don't come. "It's not like that, actually. Marie's dead," he finally blurts.

"I have heard that. My, my... what could possibly have possessed her to do that, Mason? What have you gotten yourself into since we last talked?"

"Look, things did not go as planned, and I've made a mistake, a big one, and I am in a bind. I just need some time. To sort things out."

"You have these moments right now. What do you think you will do?"

"I can't think right now. That's the problem. I need time, away. Yes. If I could just be away and have time to figure that out. That's all I need." He almost said, "Please," but he could not bring himself to say it. Not even now.

"Your first choice should be to take responsibility for your mistake... or not."

"Well that won't work! It just isn't that simple."

"It is always that simple. You are such a fool, Mason." His face reddens. "Your problem is that no one ever taught you about responsibility. It is the problem with families like yours, Mason. It is not the wealth. It is believing that control is and should be in your hands. It is imagining that you can escape the consequences of your choices. Eventually, everything balances. This is your opportunity to be accountable."

He stood up. "Well, that's just great! You are lecturing me! You're the one making backroom deals. You're the one wanting a casino so you can get rich like everyone else. How dare you lecture me?!"

"I think you might want to sit back down, Mason. It may be a while."

"A while for what?" As he spoke, from the loft, down the staircase, comes the handsome young men from the ball. No tuxedos. No masks, but he recognizes their bearing. He had not paid any attention to them at the ball, but here, in close quarters, he could see that they were able, and one of them has a Winchester riding on his arm.

"For the sheriff to arrive. I'm sure they are on their way. Do you think that I am without communication because I do not have a cell phone? I don't need television or phones to know what is going on in Moluku. Our eyes and ears are everywhere. This is the land of the People. We know what you and your sister have done. And now there is only you. So, please, take a seat. Relax." He turned his head to the door. "Don't recommend that. Take a seat, Mason."

He looks around again to realize the men are now downstairs; he hears the slam of the rifle moving a shell into its chamber. It is lowered, not pointed at him. Yet. This is no answer. It's a trap. He's boiling, but he sits.

"You see, Mason, I told you, if you didn't fix your first mess, we would be back to collect your debt. I will take your surrender and accountability as payment in full. And in so doing, I make clear to you that we never implied or endorsed your choices. Your plan was ill-conceived from the beginning. But you brought it to us, and we were willing to see if you could pull it off. You see nothing. You understand nothing. And now our business is concluded. Is that clear?"

Mason's head turns again as the headlights of three vehicles turn into the property. One BCS and two MLPD. Kapá nods, and one of the men goes to the door, opens it, and steps out.

Sheriff Noble and Lieutenant Riley exit their vehicle, weapons in their hands at their sides, and look up at the door to see a young Maidu standing, waiting. The sheriff looks at Riley; she nods and walks toward the pinecone, putting her weapon away. "I am here to make sure my mother is OK." She nods and smiles.

The young man steps to the side and indicates she should enter. "Kapá is here. She has something you want." He knows who she is.

Riley feels relieved, smiles, turns and nods to the sheriff.

Sheriff Noble holsters his weapon and tells himself that it is inappropriate to enjoy this. But buried deep inside, where even he cannot access the file, part of him knows this is going to be fun.

"A lot of paperwork. The chief and his team can handle most of it."

"Storm made all the difference."

"Yes. They couldn't get that body out of the Sierras. If they'd have made it to 395, or worse, once on 395, if they'd have made it to the Mojave Desert, even they probably wouldn't have been able to find it once they buried it, even just dumped it. A naked body, left in the Mojave... Well, food chain. It'd have been lost."

"Mason doesn't have his sister to rely on, family cut him loose. Bet he didn't figure that. He's toast."

"If he'd had the conviction of his sister, he'd have done himself like she did, but he is a gutless weasel, after all his bluster, his bullish ways. It always amazes me what is behind big fronts, big acts."

"It's the fluff-up strategy," Riley said, laughing.

"What?"

"My mother says that birds, especially the ones that make their nest on the ground, do that. They fluff up their feathers, bluster to make predators think they are bigger and fiercer than they really are to scare them away from the nest. It's protection. Really fierce creatures are sleek and more confident. A puma might sneak up on you and pounce, but they don't pretend to be fierce. They are fierce. It's always the frightened little birds that fluff up." Then they could not completely stifle the spontaneous chortles.

"Hyoid bone and DNA. I'd say he's going away for a long time."

"And we have Betsy. She saw the bruises. She can identify Dawson. They're both finished."

"And Howard Billings will keep Betsy safe and strong."

"Yeah. I heard. I feel bad for his family."

"Yes. He has a mess. He'll end up resigning."

"Over an affair?"

"There's more. He's a good man. But he just stepped a little over the line and look what happened."

"Sorry to hear that. At least Mason won't get away with it."

"Marie did. I just have the feeling that on balance, she was OK with how it all turned out."

"Really? She's dead. As dead as Malloy," Jason queried.

"There must have been satisfaction in pulling that trigger on Logan Malloy. I think the whole thing was like some giant pressure valve for her, and when she pulled the trigger on herself, it was somehow a release, maybe..." she is searching for the words to convey a momentary expression, "... a relief, no. Some climactic gratification. I can't explain it entirely. It was the way she looked at that moment. I can still see her face."

"Maybe. But all of them. With the limitless possibilities, this is what they created for themselves. It's pathetic.

"How could a family pass on a legacy of callous horror, greed, and corruption? For that matter, how could a town be so perverse, Jason?"

Jason smiles as he hears the use of his first name, and it pleases him a great deal. "Maybe sociopathy gets handed down like any other trait, disorder, disease. Way above my pay grade. As to the town, there are good people there. They are not all bad. Got to be careful of judging them all based on the ones that we run into in our line of work."

"But even the Police Chief, Betsy Hall—they all had secrets and were cheating."

"Howard just got himself caught in one of the oldest traps in the history of humankind. He married a woman he didn't really love. Eventually, he comes across the one he loved however, it was too late to avoid ruining lives. And Betsy, well, she played a dangerous game and got really stung. They're not as bad as they are foolish."

"Even Eli Lucas. He tried to thwart us at every turn. You'd think he'd recognize the importance of getting to the truth. Even my mother was involved in her own way. Everyone was dirty to one degree or the other."

"Lauren," Jason replies, "be careful. It is easy in our line of work to convert what we deal with to bitterness about everyone. In fact, it's a hazard for law enforcement to become jaded. I don't want to preach, but for someone like you, smart and capable, well, I don't want you to go astray. So, listen to me very carefully."

He allows himself to settle in a bit, to look squarely into the dark clarity of her eyes and enjoy her beauty at the same time that he is deciding he does not want to take a first misstep. He permits his face to soften: Jason speaking to the lovely Lauren, "In all of life, it is the people who get all the notoriety—often the ones we deal with. People that do disgraceful things, even bad cops. Bad politicians, celebrities, lawyers, people from all walks of life. These are the headlines, big noise. And often, it is because these sorts of people have a forum and tend to hold themselves up—as if they have some charter to set the rest of us straight on one thing or the other. Hell, we do it for them. Face it. We tend to look up to them. Pander after their choices, values.

"All of that is what sells newspapers, television advertisements, social media networks. It's ordinary, decent lives that really matter but don't make headlines. It is garbage being sold to the public for profit and for control by even worse people behind the scenes. They are powerful, but they are not the majority."

He wants to touch her, take her hand, but he does not. He pauses, holding in that compulsion. "Recognize that for every one of the scum we deal with, there are a thousand ordinary, genuine, real folks. They are also from all walks of life. Some of them have wealth. Some of them do not. Some intelligent, some not so much. But they all work hard, try to do the right thing, make mistakes, learn, carry on, and they are who we are. Every time you come across scum, remember, you are choosing to stand between that scum and the thousands of ordinary, genuine real folk, the majority, those we swore to protect and serve. Keep your eyes and your heart there, and you'll be OK." And then he does not hold back, "I want you to be OK, better than OK, Lauren." Jason Noble begins to realize that his caring for this woman is on a precipice.

Lauren hears her name, seeing the face of Jason Noble reaching into her in the only way he can, with his mind, his heart. It generates warm sensations at her core. She feels the preciousness of this moment more than she gives it thought. It can last forever, but it cannot, and she pulls back from the brink of feeling. She is loaded with new information on many levels and resumes her reasoning of all that has happened.

She melds her mother's words with Sheriff Noble's words. She can feel the canker in herself. Anger. An overwhelming disgust for what she has just witnessed. Was it her European genes festering with resentment? Was it her people? Her mother had always said it is better not to judge. But Kapá does judge. Often and profoundly. She would say she measures. But isn't that the same thing?

Lauren admires her People. But she also recognizes that they have made mistakes. The simplicity of their life before the Europeans makes them seem virtuous. Yet not all of them were pure, are pure. They made mistakes; they make mistakes today. The people are not perfect.

It is also simplistic to presume that the canker is the European. Maybe there is a canker in all humans. She wants to heal that canker in herself and not let it gnaw away. She wants to go to the safest, warmest, lightest place on Earth. She imagines Kapá in her pinecone, digesting all that has happened. The thought makes her smile, and she imagines what her mother would have to say. She wonders what Kapá would say about Jason Noble. Jason. She decides another time.

Instead, she drives up Olive Highway, across the Feather River and toward Berry Creek, takes the cutoff, and heads to Bald Rock. Not so much snow at this elevation. The Rock is icy and a cautious climb. Out on the edge of that giant piece of granite, she looks across the Sacramento Valley to the horizon, the coastal range. This was the land of the People. She thinks of the past. Decides it should be left as it fell.

She has to be brave and find her own path. Looking out over the vast land, she feels a light inside her being at her solar plexus. It is bright and growing, and it consumes her until, in the cold, fresh air, she is warmed. But it grows even more and engulfs the entire valley, the entire vista. She feels every leaf, every creature, every drop of water, and the weight of every rock, of Earth. But she is not overwhelmed. She is secure in the sense of belonging that she experiences and does not realize her arms are outstretched as if to welcome it all into her soul.

Melody and words dance in her mind as she looks out at the valley. "... *purple mountains majesty, above the fruited plain...*" "*This is my home. I am a child of these mountains, this rich valley. And its history. No one's history is spotless. If it were, there would be no opportunity for learning,*" she thought. "*The best any of us can hope for is the prospect of learning until our last day on Earth.*"

No new snow today. Roads are open. On the far horizon, there is a strip of bright blue sky and hints of the sun in the west shining through like great shards of light. Lauren knows that she is patient like the earth itself, and she has faith that like the earth, like nature, everything balances forever and always. For the night, there is day. For pain, there is joy. For life, there is death. For evil, there is good. Over time, all in equal measure. And this, too, is learning. She inhales into her being what her mother had told her about the scales of the universe.

It dawns on the young lieutenant that the real battle she has chosen is the battle to keep her balance—in a complicated world. There will never be easy answers, but there are right choices every day. Even if selected from lesser, trickier options, there is always the right choice for her.

15

MILES AWAY . . .

The sun is rising behind them and casting diamonds on the Tyrrhenian Sea. It is early spring, so the weather is cool, and the season has not begun to flourish. Purple and lavender buds of wisteria are visible on the hillsides, in courtyards, hanging from the arbors and baskets, but they have yet to open. Compared to the Sierra Nevada, it is warm and pleasant.

The terrace looks out to the sea and has a view of the curving, steep hillside covered with picturesque villas stepping up the cliffs. The smell of saltwater, wet earth, and coffee hang in the humid air. The storm clouds to the far southwest indicate there'll be rain again, in the next day or so. But this morning, is perfection.

"Tell the truth, did you know it was Marie all along?"

"I was sure she was behind it." Atticus sips espresso. "Before I left town, I told her what Logan was going to do, what she had found. I even embellished. Knew it would drive her crazy."

Jayden paused, recognizing the implication of what her heard. "So, in a way, it was you. Your weapon was Marie's need for respectability and admiration. You knew that she would take out your adversary if properly primed."

"Yes and no. I thought she would call her uncle, and he would send a fixer, like he had in the past when there were *problems* for the family. I figured they'd pinch Malloy up, threaten her, buy her rag for some obscene amount of money, bribe her. Something like that. "

"She could have cranked up Mason. How did you know it wasn't him?"

"No. Marie would not trust Mason to do anything of that magnitude. In fact, think about it. If Mason had left Elyse James to Marie, this might have been one unsolved crime and a few waves to negotiate."

"Elyse? You believe Mason killed her?"

"Probably. The cops believe it, too. By the time we return home, they'll catch Mason up if they haven't already. He is clumsy and stupid." Atticus sips his espresso. "Although I clearly wanted Logan out of my way, I must confess, it never occurred to me that Marie would do the proverbial *wet work* herself. So atypical for her. That was a surprise. Delightful, really."

"And tried to hang it on you."

"Yes. Well, that was no great shock. Not really. Perhaps we were both exhausted of the pretense. That's when I knew for sure it was Marie. Using one from my collection of weapons was probably a misstep on her part. It brought it to her doorstep as well as mine. Too close."

"She should have tracked your flight closer."

"Yes." Atticus laughs robustly. "I imagine the whole thing would have been quite difficult if not for the last-minute delay of that flight and then that endless drive! I almost stayed over in the city—but then I didn't have to drive in that snow. She miscalculated." Shrugging. "Costly."

"You don't think it was about you and your, shall we say, *alfresco* predilections?"

"Marie preferred a marriage that placed no sexual pressure on her. She certainly never loved me or anyone, I'd guess. And I, well, I loved her money, of course. Very fond of the money, endless supply. It is, after all, how I built my empire. And it will now be, well, finite. But significant." Another sip. "She was a handsome woman. But alas... Decades ago, the veil of propriety—it was most useful. It suited us both very well at the time."

"Being referred to as the 'short end of a lavender marriage' would have been utterly repulsive, I imagine," Jayden says with a careless chuckle.

"Humiliating—if it were definitively known. No more enviable grand entrances and the perfect power couple, kiss on the hand, all that. And I am sure it would have kindled fire inside her otherwise glacial existence. But she was a master at living behind masks. And together, we could have weathered that scandal."

"It would have been messy."

He smiles, barely raising an eyebrow and the corner of his mouth, continuing, "But here's the thing, dear, sweet boy, I'm not sure that I cared at all about it. By the time Logan started the threats, I don't think I wanted to weather anything. I preferred to make it go away. Don't misunderstand, Logan Malloy had become overly annoying in general. *Her*—and her lust for power—thinking she could accost, well, me, was more objectionable than her little scandals. They were just tedious."

"Well, I rather enjoyed being the talk of the town."

"Yes. And believe me, you will still! Frankly, even this messy inconvenience is good for business. At least for a while."

"But that casino will happen."

"Yes. Inevitable. None of us really cared about the casino. It was all about power and control. Logan, like most of us, just wanted power." He adjusts his cup on the saucer as he places it on the table. "Actually, I grow weary of Moluku Lake. I might sell my shares to Eli." Atticus let that news settle on the morning. "I find it amusing to imagine Grace Lucas rising to the status of Queen of Eagle's Nest." He cannot contain a small bit of laughter.

"I'd say, sensing that I just didn't care about Logan's juicy story, is why she started digging for something else in the first place. When she tied into the notorious Black Carnation, she bit off more than she was prepared to chew. I knew that she had handed me the means to cripple her for good. Her fatal mistake was going after the Oeillets! That was never going to happen. They are impervious!"

"Yes. And apparently, they have a vicious streak," Jayden laughs; Atticus nods, smiling. "Poor, dear Marie," Jayden feigns sympathy. "I wonder if anyone realizes that, after all, it really was you that caused both Marie's demise and Logan's death."

"And that foolish little tart reporter. What's her name again?"

"Elyse James."

"Yes. Oh, and the downfall of the beastly Mason. I want all my points." Chuckling and jolly.

"You are truly, dastardly cunning! And something else... callously vengeful, I think."

As those words hang on the morning air, Atticus smiles with amused gratification. An artist always enjoys appreciation of his work. No one else is going to admire this bit of art, so he allows himself to bathe in it.

Jayden Listeri turns his face to the distant clouds on the horizon. More rain. Day or two at the most. He is both contemplative and wary. Then, back again to his partner, "You are just a little scary. You know that?"

Atticus turns to look straight at Jayden. He has just a hint of that smile remaining on his face. But his bright blue eyes were twinkling with pleasure. "Shall we go to Venice before we return?" he asks disarmingly.

"No, it's sinking, and frankly, it smells. Pity. I love it so. But I agree. Let's go somewhere. Capri or Athens?"

"Athens, then. Yes. Shame about the sinking," Atticus says with a flourish of his hand.

"Athens! Mykonos! And Santorini! We can ferry to the island. Perfect," Jayden exclaims.

"Now that's a fire in the belly of the ocean," Atticus says with demure passion.

"And you... you are... a volcano, too, I think. I saw this article, on the internet or television, somewhere. Not really my thing. But curiously, there's some moon, I think, around some planet somewhere, spewing ice into space. That's you, I think. You are a volcano of ice!"

They both inhale and burst into laughter.

Made in the USA
Columbia, SC
26 August 2022

65724126R00122